Harlequin
Presents..

Other titles by

VIOLET WINSPEAR
IN HARLEQUIN PRESENTS

VIOLET WINSPEAR

dearest demon

Harlequin Books

TORONTO • LONDON • NEW YORK • AMSTERDAM • SYDNEY • WINNIPEG

Harlequin Presents edition published February 1976
SBN 373-70630-8

Original hard cover edition published in 1975
by Mills & Boon Limited

CHAPTER ONE

THERE came a hazing of all shadows that elongated as the sun fell with a streaking, flaming beauty and the sky deepened to purple-blue. The scene had an unreal quality, so that Destine wondered if she was dreaming or really travelling by train through the flame-tinged fields and valleys, past high-walled farms and the ruins of old castles.

Darkness came suddenly, as she had been warned that it would in this region that was almost tropical, and it saddened her to lose sight of the towering palm-trees and the high jagged crest of the mountains of Santa de Leones.

She would have preferred to travel during the day to her destination, but it had been impossible to book a comfortable seat on one of the day trains or a long-distance bus. They were always crowded, the Condesa had told her, and Destine hadn't argued with a woman who had lived in this country for twenty years, who before her marriage to a Spaniard had been a close friend of Destine's mother.

It was because of the Condesa that she was installed in this night train compartment, that was almost Victorian in its padded comfort and its seclusion, the blinds to the corridor drawn down so that she had complete privacy from other passengers. She would have preferred to see other people passing to and fro, but the Condesa had said that it was better for a woman travelling alone in the south to keep to herself.

Destine was a trained nurse and up until now she had always worked in hospitals; now for the first time she was going to work privately for a friend of her godmother's. A woman who had lost the use of her legs after an attack of

5

polio, which had struck her down while she had been on her honeymoon. A short while afterwards her husband had left her and it was thought that he had gone away with another woman; as a result she had fallen into a melancholia that so alarmed her family that at the Condesa's suggestion they had agreed to hire an English nurse for her, one who could come all the way to Santa de Leones to be in constant attendance upon the Señora Arandas.

'You are exactly the right sort of person for this case,' the Condesa had written to Destine. 'You are practical, and you took so well the sadness of losing your own husband. You have something very much in common with Cosima—both of you lost something of great value on your honeymoon.'

Destine had lost her husband, a young and brilliantly promising doctor, who had been crushed to death in his car right outside the restaurant where they had stopped for a meal on their way to Cornwall. Destine had forgotten her handbag and had gone back inside to fetch it—the big Bentley had run into Matt's car during her short absence. Her husband of six hours had been killed outright, and sometimes her own single, terrible scream still rent her dreams and turned them into nightmares.

If at the time she had seemed not to show any emotion it was because it had happened so suddenly, but for a long time her grief had been deep and silent. She returned to her nursing, and friends seemed to think it best not to mention Matt. It was as if he had never been, yet there was a gold ring on her left hand to prove that he had lived and loved her.

A strange sort of coincidence did seem to underlie this coming meeting with Señora Arandas. 'It was meant to be, I think,' the Condesa had said, when she had come to the train with Destine and ensured that she had food, wine and books for the journey. 'Cosima is of a similar age to yourself, Destine, and one might also call you soul-twins.'

Destine rested her head against the padded seat and closed

her eyes, so that the rhythm of the train became soothing, hypnotic, so that she might have fallen asleep had she not been inwardly nervous about working in a strange country, among people who were foreign to her. That she knew Spanish was one of those fortunate things; when her mother had been alive they had spent several holidays with the Condesa and it had fascinated Destine to learn the language, and the Conde, that most courteous of gentlemen, had insisted that her pronunciation and her grammar be exact, and her flow of words so fluent that it would startle Latin people that so fair a woman should speak their language as if it were her own.

She smiled a little ... none of them could have guessed that her language lessons as a teenager would result in her employment by Latin people when she was a woman of twenty-four.

Then her smile faded and her face became pensive. No one could have known that this would be her future, for at nineteen she had met Matt at the teaching hospital and they had become engaged quite soon. But they had waited to marry, putting it off until he had qualified as a surgeon, and by that time Destine had been twenty-two.

It seemed incredible that it was almost two years since that awful accident ... two long and lonely years in which some of her former gaiety had lost its sparkle, and she had become a composed, efficient, and self-sufficient young career woman.

She would never marry again ... of that she was certain. Matt had meant the world to her, and never again could she feel so much a part of another human being. Her great regret was that they had never been lovers. Matt had never demanded that during the course of their engagement. He had had a fine discipline of mind, body and hand. He would, she knew, have been a great surgeon and a strong, stable husband. Their life together would have been a good one, soundly based on the security of their mutual love and respect for each other.

Love ... romance ... marriage, they were ended for her. At twenty-four Destine Chard was quite content to be excellent at her job, and to have just a few very good friends. She asked nothing more of life, not any more. Matthew was gone, and so was her dearly loved mother. She believed that the shock of the accident had weakened her mother's heart, for she had loved Matt as if he were her own son.

Destine sighed ... it didn't pay off to plan your life, for there was some strange element in it that did the planning. Like her name she was a woman of destiny ... she had not known a month ago that she would agree to come to Santa de Leones to work. When the Condesa's letter had first arrived she had been inclined to reply that under no circumstances could she think of leaving her hospital work ... when or why the decision had been reversed she couldn't say. But one evening she had found herself sitting down to reply to her godmother that she would find it a change to work abroad.

And here she was, only hours away from her first meeting with her Spanish patient, in a region of the south that the Condesa had said was hot, picturesque, and still faintly Moresque.

It was getting on for midnight when a sudden jolt of the train wheels stirred Destine out of the half-sleep into which she had fallen. She glanced at her wristwatch ... ten minutes more and they would be running into the station where she was to alight. The place was called Xanas, a Spanish word that meant fabulous, enticing, part of an enchantment.

Xanas. She repeated it to herself, with the exact pronunciation. The Latin language was a colourful and difficult one, but she had mastered it when she was a schoolgirl, the best time of all to learn a second language.

She opened her handbag of golden-tan leather, which she

8

had bought in Madrid, where the Condesa and her husband had an apartment, and taking out a comb and mirror she tidied her hair, which took a simple cut and needed only a couple of strokes of the comb to look right. She was naturally fair, and the streak of silver running from her temple to her nape was not there to add a dash of glamour to her appearance. It had been there since Matt had died; the result of the shock she had suffered when she had run from the restaurant to find a shattered body in place of the lean, clever-faced man she had married in church only hours before the tragic ending of his life.

The man responsible had been driving recklessly, in a temper, hurtling the big car out of the way of a cat running across the forecourt of the restaurant. In that split second he had crashed into the smaller car that was parked there, waiting for Destine. Murderer! She had flung the word in the face of the man who had killed her husband and all her hopes for the future, and she would always remember the sudden terrible look in his eyes.

She had been too ill to attend the inquest, where it had been established that the unfortunate appearance of the cat on the drive, and the rather dangerous way in which the dead man had been parked, had combined to cause an accident not due in any way to drink or faulty steering. The case had closed on a note of regret, certain costs, and that was all.

But from that moment Destine seemed to hate men. She couldn't endure their touch, or the compliments that were aimed in their own self-interest. When a man flirted with her, she just looked at him with chilly blue eyes; a girl who changed overnight into a cool and untouchable woman, kind towards her patients, but whose emotions were iced over.

Satisfied that she looked neat and tidy even after a fairly long journey, Destine gathered her belongings together, and tried to ignore the slight fluttering of nerves in her midriff. She was usually very composed, but this was the first time

9

she had arrived in a strange place at midnight, to take on a case that the Condesa had warned was going to be a difficult one.

The Señora Arandas had not adjusted to her life as an invalid, nor had she forgotten the man who had walked out on her; who had not stood by her now she could no longer be the full and vibrant woman she had been.

Men! Destine muttered the word to herself as the train ran smoothly into the station, where ringed by lights was the name of the region, Xanas.

She was the only passenger to alight on the platform that was deep with shadow where the lights didn't penetrate, and she stood a moment feeling almost a sense of panic that made her want to jump back on the train. But that would be a foolish and childish thing to do; it would be letting down her patient, and her godmother, who had said quite frankly that Destine had needed a change of environment for a long time now.

She lifted her suitcase as the train began to move off without her; too late now to run away, and with abrupt resignation she made for the station office, where a sleepy porter accepted her ticket and mumbled that no one with a car waited for the Señora Chaid. Perhaps she would care to take a seat while she waited? As he said this he cast a curious look over her slim, impeccable figure in a pale, tailored trouser-suit. That she was a foreigner was obvious, but he was puzzled, she knew, that she should speak his language so well.

'I'll wait outside and stretch my legs,' she said. 'I've had a long journey, and I don't suppose I shall have to wait very long for a car to come and fetch me.'

'Will the *señora* be staying at the *posada*?' he asked, with that natural and uninhibited curiosity of the country Latin.

'No, I am to go to the Casera de las Rejas,' she explained. 'I am the new nurse for the *dueña* there.'

10

'The *dueña*?' He looked faintly puzzled. 'Is she sick, then? We had not heard that this was so.'

'I'm speaking of the Señora Arandas,' Destine explained. She's an invalid – '

'Ah, but of course.' He looked relieved. 'We are all very fond of our Marquesa and we shouldn't wish to hear that she was sick.'

'The Marquesa?' It was Destine's turn to look perplexed. 'I do have the correct address, I hope? The Señora Arandas does reside at the Casera de las Rejas?'

'*Absolutamente*,' he replied. 'She is the daughter of the Marquesa – did you not know?'

Destine frowned and wondered why the Condesa had not mentioned this fact. Had she thought that working for a titled family might put Destine off ... it all rushed back, her fury of two years ago; her insistence that the court had been lenient with the murderer of Matt because he had been titled. An Honourable Something-or-Other. Highly dishonourable in the unrelenting opinion of Destine; he had used influence and money to get him off the hook that she would have liked to thrust in his throat, she hated him so much.

'Well, so long as I have the right address,' she said, pulling herself together. 'I've come a long way and should hate to be stranded – '

'I hear a vehicle, *señora*, so it would seem that you have come to the right place.' The porter smiled sleepily, and followed her out of the office into the slightly chill air of the station. Regions that were hot during the daytime were invariably cool at night, and Destine gave a slight shiver as she felt the touch of the wind, and saw in the dimness the approaching vehicle that was bound to be for her. Hoofs clattered on the cobbles of the station forecourt and a horse-drawn landau appeared, looking so old-world and far removed from the modern way of life that Destine felt a

11

curious sense of being in another world, in another time, so that she ought to be wearing a chip-bonnet and a hoop skirt instead of a suit.

A man leapt down noiselessly from the landau and the lights were too dim out here for Destine to be able to make out his face. She presumed that he was a servant from the *casa,* for there was no one else for him to be meeting at this time of the night.

'You are the Señora Chard from Madrid?' he asked.

'That is so.' He was an exceptionally tall man and she had to tilt her head to look at him, though she was no dwarf herself. She had an impression of hair so black that it was almost invisible in the shadows, and she caught the gleam of eyes equally dark. Again she shivered, for no certain reason, and when he reached for her suitcase she felt half inclined to hold on to it, and not go with him. His height unnerved her, and the dark aloofness of him as he was briefly close to her, unlocking her hold on the case.

'Have you no other luggage?' he asked, and her brows gathered in a frown at his peremptory way of addressing her. She had heard from other nurses that servants didn't always take kindly to the presence of a nurse in the house. She was neither a servant herself, nor a guest, and Destine had a sudden cold feeling that she had made a mistake in coming here. She shouldn't have listened to her godmother and been persuaded that it would help heal old wounds if she left England and came to Xanas for a few months.

'I have a small trunk that is being sent on separately,' she said, in a reluctant voice.

'Then let us be away—'

'You are from the Casera de los Rejas?' Suspicion tinged her voice, and a thread of uncertainty. 'You are the chauffeur for the family?'

As she said this Destine heard the station porter catch his breath quite audibly; she thought he was about to speak, but

12

the man who had come to fetch her shot a look at him that was sufficient to still the words on his lips. This little exchange so increased Destine's sense of foreboding that she actually reached out as if to take back her suitcase. Her fingers came in contact with his hand, and as if burned she drew away.

'Come!' He spoke with a tinge of impatience. 'It is a late enough hour for a nurse to arrive at Xanas without the necessity of wasting further time. I am from the *casa* where your patient awaits you, so there is no need to regard me as Count Dracula about to carry you away to a bat's belfry.'

'Really!' Destine had not had very much to do with Latin servants, but it seemed to her that this man was extremely insolent. It was because she was the nurse, of course. Had she been a guest of the family his manner would have been a bit more deferential, and she followed him to the old-fashioned conveyance with the unhappy feeling that nursing in a private house was going to be a lot different from working in a hospital. There one was part of a team instead of being all alone and at the mercy of hostile servants, the possible interference of the family and the moody disposition of the invalid herself.

Destine tried not to jerk away like a nervous schoolgirl when the driver put a hand beneath her elbow in order to assist her into the landau. *'Gracias.'* She sat down quickly in her seat and watched covertly as he leapt up at the other side and took the reins. The harness jingled as the horse trotted out of the station yard on to the dark road that lay ahead of them. She had known that Xanas was a country place, but hadn't quite imagined it in the depths of beyond. The village, for there had to be one, probably lay in the other direction, for they passed no habitations for some considerable time, and everything was silent but for the regular beat of the hoofs on the road.

The lights of the vehicle illumined only the road ahead

13

of them, so that Destine still had no clear impression of the man at her side. They seemed to be driving through fields of some tall plant that rustled like straw, and finally she had to break the silence, for if these were wheat fields, then never had she seen wheat that grew so high.

'Sugar cane,' he said in answer to her question. 'This region has a hot sun and is sheltered by the mountains, so many of the crops are of a tropical variety. As you are from England, *señora,* I hope you won't find our climate too sultry for you. It would be a pity to have come all this way only to find that you had made a mistake. Personally speaking I think a Spanish nurse would be more suitable.'

'I daresay.' Destine spoke with slight sarcasm. 'But I understood that a Spanish nurse—or were there several?— had not been successful in dealing with Señora Arandas. I was informed that she has bad moods of depression, and her Latin nurses were inclined to encourage her bouts of misery rather than to make her snap out of them. Tears are no use. They alter nothing, and only make a person feel more sorry for oneself.'

'You sound very cold and severe,' he said. 'I am relieved that I am not to be your patient if you are so unsympathetic.'

'Of course I have sympathy for people who are sick, otherwise I wouldn't be a nurse.' Destine flushed slightly, and wondered why it was that she had got off to such a bad start with this man. If he was representative of the staff at the *casa,* then she was in for a grand time.

'I think I had better warn you,' he said, 'that the Marquesa won't take kindly to anyone being too severe with her daughter. She was popular and vivacious and had the promise of a good life ahead of her, only to have everything snatched away from her just as her lips were at the rim of the glass.'

'But she has her life,' Destine said quietly. 'She has that to be thankful for, and I might add that I have never been

14

unkind to a patient; I have come here only with the idea of helping Señora Arandas to adjust to a different sort of life. Some victims of polio lose the entire use of their body, but she can use her arms, and she can take breath without the aid of a breathing machine. You must admit that she has more chance of making a happy life than those who are totally paralysed?'

'Then let us hope that you are successful, *señora.*' His tone of voice was sardonic, and Destine shot a look at him and decided that he was one of those infuriating Latins who believed in *saudade;* of living in the past and taking punishment for not finding happiness. Infuriating to Destine because, in a manner of speaking, she also had that attitude with regard to herself. She knew it wasn't right, and she would do her utmost to shake her patient out of that frame of mind and heart, but all the same it did apply to herself. Dreams half caught at. The wine of happiness dashed from the lips. How well she understood, and must and would fight with Señora Arandas to abandon her ghosts and let the future guide her out of the shadows of self-pity and loss of confidence in her womanhood.

'Have we much farther to go?' She wasn't going to argue with someone who disapproved of her appointment as nurse at the Casera de los Rejas, and who seemed to think that it was better to let the invalid dwell in the past. She could only hope that she wouldn't see too much of him . . . no doubt he was employed to drive the Marquesa about in this quaint mode of transport, for the Condesa had often said that the Latin aristocracy had a tendency to live as their forebears had lived.

'Another mile or so,' he replied, in an uncompromising tone of voice. 'It is a very Spanish establishment, *señora,* in a very isolated region of Spain, and no concessions of any sort will be made for someone from England, who is accustomed to the potted amusements of television and the discotheque. The *casa* is built on the lines of a Moorish house, for long ago this region was in the hands of the Moors. It was they who brought the palm tree and the oleander, the azulejos, and the water garden. In the veins of most who dwell here in Xanas there runs a strong vein of the desert, and a liking for high walls that keep out the hot winds and the intruder.'

'Do you regard me as an intruder?' Destine felt sure that he did, and though she also felt compelled to ask him what business it was of his, she kept back the words. There was something about him that forbade insolence, though he wasn't backward with his own sardonic remarks.

'I regard you as the new nurse and nothing more,' he said. 'It was what the Marquesa wanted in her concern for her child, and so let us hope that you have the right medicine to offer.'

'My medicine will not be too sweet, or too bitter, I can assure you of that, *señor*. I intend to do my best for Señora Arandas.'

'Let us hope your good intentions last, *señora*. The evenings can be very quiet at the *casa,* and you are young and probably accustomed to the company of the young doctors with whom you worked——'

'That is none of your business.' This time temper overruled discretion and Destine felt quite furious with this—this servant who seemed to take it upon himself to offer warnings instead of a welcome to someone who had to earn her living just as he did, and didn't want to find that she had travelled miles to an uncongenial job. How dared he suppose that she was some sort of flirt? And how unconsciously cruel he was to suggest that she amused herself with a doctor . . . she had lost the only doctor in the world for her. Now they were just white-clad models of cleverness and efficiency; if they had charm it failed to melt the ice around her heart.

'You appear to have a temper,' he drawled. 'By all

16

means use it on me, but none of us permit the Marquesa to be upset.'

'I wouldn't dream of upsetting her,' Destine gasped. 'You seem to have formed a very low opinion of me, *señor*.'

'Perhaps we have formed a low opinion of each other, *señora*. The midnight hour can have an odd effect upon the sensibilities, for it is the enchanter's hour, is it not?'

'Yes,' she agreed, and cast a perplexed glance at his shadowed profile. 'The hour of bells, bats and ghosts – you would be annoyed at having to turn out so late in order to meet a nurse whom you consider is wasting her time and everyone else's in coming here. Your scepticism is disheartening, *señor*.'

'I just don't want you to think that I am driving you to a fool's paradise, *señora*. A post in southern Spain could be regarded by some as a vacation rather than a vocation, could it not?'

'It never entered my head to regard this post as a sort of holiday in Spain,' she said indignantly. 'You seem to have a prejudiced view of English people, as if we are all after a good time and don't care at whose expense we get it! I am not one of that number, thank you!'

'Time will tell,' he said sardonically. 'You won't last long at the Casa de las Rejas if you are just another glamorous blonde on the hunt for a rich protector, dazzled by your fair skin and your phoney hair – '

'My what?' Destine could hardly believe that she had heard him correctly. In all her life no one had ever suggested that her flaxen hair was unnatural, and here was this – this servant suggesting that she dyed it!

'It is out of a bottle, of course,' he said. 'I caught a glimpse of your hair by the station lights – no woman could be so naturally fair, and I believe the fashion started in Hollywood, did it not? To think that Hollywood was once part of the Spanish empire in California!'

17

'You're the absolute limit!' Destine informed him, a blaze to her blue eyes that for so long had been cool as an English down. 'Who the devil do you think you are to talk to me in such a fashion? I shall report you to the Marquesa for your insolence—I'm sure she wouldn't be pleased if she knew how you speak to—to—'

'Were you going to say "guests"?' he drawled. 'A Freudian slip of the tongue, *señora*. Did I not say that no English girl who has such a chic face and figure, not to mention the hair, would come to Spain merely to waste herself on an invalid woman?'

'Yes, you did say it,' Destine spoke furiously, 'but it doesn't happen to be true. I have about as much interest in flirting with men as that—that horse has! I'm a widow—'

'I had been informed, *señora*. English widows, unlike Latin ones, don't take to the black mantilla—though in your case the hair would look quite ravishing under the black lace.'

'How dare you?' Destine felt a cold dash of shock following on her hot wave of fury. 'I fully intend to report you to the Marquesa. I can't wait!'

'Neither can I!' he drawled, and at that precise moment the landau took a swerve around a bend in the road and there was a sudden gush of scent as they sped beneath a tunnel of jasmine. Jasmine! Like a burst of tiny stars, arching over twin walls that seemed to be part of a long arcade. The abrupt realisation that they had almost arrived at the *casa* was a distraction that took Destine's mind off the man at her side—for the moment, at least. They came to the end of the arcade and swept in under a great archway, past the towering girths of palm trees and great cascades of flowering vine. The air was alive with a mixture of perfumes, distilled by the coolness of night after the heat of the day that kept the essences of the flowers locked away. Now they were released with an almost flagrant abandon, and there at the centre of the enclosed patio was the glimmering

18

alabaster shape of a fountain, shut off right now to preserve the water that was precious in the south, so that the figures that held the basins were like pale ghosts in the light of lanterns attached by wrought-iron to the white walls.

Destine's first impression was of a noble old *casa,* rambling around the huge patio, and towering into several galleries, with iron-screened balconies.

The House of the Grilles. Rampant with tropical flowers and trees . . . remote and Moresque . . . enclosing a family cloistered against the modern world from which Destine had come.

The man who had driven her to the *casa* leapt down to the tiles of the patio with that silent litheness she had noticed before. He extended a hand to assist her, and she supposed that he was so accustomed to the elderly Marquesa that he took it for granted she would need his help in alighting.

'I can manage, thank you,' she said, and couldn't quite understand her reaction against his touch. She believed had he tried to reach for her hand she would have leapt from the other side of the vehicle.

He merely shrugged his shoulders and took her suitcase, leaving her to alight on her own. She glanced about her, seeing once again the way the ground-floor rooms were arranged around the courtyard, each with an oval carved entrance revealed by the wall lanterns.

Her escort approached one of these entrances, and then turned to see if she followed him . . . Destine caught her breath for in that instant the light of one of the lanterns fell upon his face and she saw haughty, well-marked features and forceful brows sheltering the incredibly dark eyes. The pride of that hawk-like face wasn't all that struck Destine dumb, nor that slight twist to the mouth that suggested a cynical man. Not even the terrible scar that jagged across the left side of his face, adding to his somewhat sinister look, was enough in itself to drain all the blood from her own face and make her feel that she was going to fall to the ground in a faint.

'You!' she whispered, though she felt as if she cried it to the rooftops of the *casa*. Cried it for all ears as she had once, long ago in a nightmare, cried it in another forecourt with English oaks as sentinels instead of tall palm trees.

He stared at her, not comprehending her look, and why her blue eyes so wildly accused him.

'You,' she said again, 'or am I going mad?'

'May I say, *señora*, that I haven't the slightest comprehension of what you are talking about.' He moved and the lantern light slid off his face, leaving it masked again by shadows, the scar concealed and the deep arching of the black brows above the dark eyes and the hawkish nose. But she knew him ... she knew him ... for his face had haunted her restless sleep too long for recognition not to be mutual.

'Don't pretend,' she cried out. 'It was you who killed my husband!'

'*Dios mio!*' A thread of shock ran in his deep voice. 'You are that woman, the one whose husband died when the car of my cousin ran into his car ... was it three ... no, it was two years ago! *Ay, que pena!* What do I say?'

'Are you saying it wasn't you?' Destine felt she hated him even more for not having the courage to admit to his guilt. 'I saw you, and I shan't forget your face to my last day ... at least, then, you didn't have the scar. I suppose you got that in another crash that possibly killed someone else!'

'I was scarred as a youth,' he said. 'I have been called Don Cicatrice for as long as I can remember – it was my cousin, *señora*, who was at the wheel of the car that killed your husband. The Marqués Vincent de Obregon – Manolito, my cousin. Son of the Marquesa, brother of the woman you have come here to nurse – did no one tell you, *señora*? Did you come to the Casera de las Rejas in total ignorance of these facts? It really is incredible!'

20

Manolito, Marqués Vincent de Obregon—yes, that had been the name of the reckless foreigner who had killed Matt. How could she ever forget it? And yet how was it possible that this man with the scar was so much like him? That black hair, those dark eyes, the high cheekbones and the mouth that seemed almost chiselled!

'First cousins, *señora*, are often much alike,' he said. 'Manolito and I might almost have been taken for twins, but for this cicatrice that I carry on my face. I am known as Don Cicatrice—my actual name is Artez Dominquin y Amador Robles. My mother was sister to the Marquesa; she died when I was born and I was brought up in this house, side by side with Manolito. Many might not have told us apart, but I had this scar, and only you, *señora*, a stranger to Xanas, would mistake me for my cousin. The rest of Xanas knows that Manolito died in the bullring about a year ago. It was one of his pleasures, the baiting of the bull. It was one of his curses—to die at the age of thirty-four. It is said in Xanas that there is a curse on the Obregon family, and events would seem to bear out this belief. Would you not say?'

He waited tall and silent for Destine to answer him. All she could think of was that he looked like Manolito, and her godmother must have known this when she had arranged this post for her. Why . . . why in heaven's name had she done such a thing? How could Destine's ghosts ever rest if each time she looked at this man called Don Cicatrice she saw the almost living image of Matt's killer?

'I—I can't stay here,' she said wildly. 'You'll have to take me back to the station so I can catch a train back to Madrid—'

'There won't be another train until tomorrow,' he said. 'Tonight you must stay here—'

'No,' she shook her head, 'take me to the village, anywhere—I won't sleep under the roof of *that* man—'

21

'Manolito is dead, and you can't pass on the blame for what he did to those who are innocent of his deeds. It will help no one if you behave in this hysterical fashion—'

'You—I've had enough of you and your insulting remarks,' she flung at him. 'On the way here you called me an adventuress, and you said that my hair was dyed!'

'Ah, did I upset your vanity,' he asked sardonically. 'Do you hate me for that?'

'I hate you and all your clan,' she said bitterly. 'I'd never have come here had I known—oh, what on earth made the Condesa do this to me? What possessed her—?'

'The devil, perhaps?' He moved back silently into the lantern light and his own face looked devilish as the jagged cicatrice sprang into view again, outlining the left cheekbone as if a claw had been dragged through his flesh. 'You come to us as Señora Chard, yet was not the Englishman who died called Mitchell—Mathias Mitchell?'

'Matthew,' she corrected him stiffly. 'Mitchell was my married name, but when I returned to my nursing I kept to my single name. It was too much to bear—too much a reminder of Matthew to be called by his name almost every minute of the day. Oh, God, what am I going to do?'

'Tonight you must stay here,' he said. 'We are a long way from the village, and it is now well past midnight. The morning will soon come.'

She glanced at the *casa* with eyes that hated it. Only one or two lights could be seen beyond the ornately grilled windows . . . iron wrought into lacelike patterns to enclose the secrets and the hurts of the Obregon family. Why had the Condesa done this to her? Had she thought that Destine should face people whose troubles were akin to her own— even, in a way, more tragic than her own?

'Let us go in,' said Don Cicatrice, and there was nothing else that Destine could do but follow him into the House of the Grilles. Tonight she was at the mercy of the hour, but as soon as the morning came she would return to England.

'You will drive me to the station as soon as it's light?' she said. 'I can't stay here—I couldn't face it! Seeing you every day! You're too much like him—it's like seeing the devil resurrected!'

'Is it?' He turned briefly to look at her and his lips moved in a silght smile . . . a smile that didn't reach his dark eyes.

CHAPTER TWO

LAMPS had been supplied, but their light didn't penetrate into the far corners of the bedroom. There was electricity, he had told her, but it was turned off after ten o'clock in order to preserve the supply in the estate generator. They were too isolated for the local supply to be run this far, even for the Marquesa.

When he said that there had again been that brief and cynical smile on his lips, as if very little had the power to deeply amuse him.

Destine glanced about the room and saw the Crucifixion above the bed, with its plain white cover and tall carved posts from which was suspended the yards of netting to be drawn around the bed when it was occupied. This was a hot region and already the oil-lamps had attracted the attention of several large moths that buzzed around the globes and cast their winged shadows over the white walls.

Always the white walls and the monk-dark shadows, thought Destine. They were almost a symbol of the Latin temperament, with no half-shades. There was no indecision of features or personality. The men were devils, or they were saints. The women were mothers, or they were nuns. It was a temperament that had its fascination . . . and its fearfulness.

The long windows were draped in old-gold brocade from which the design had long faded. The lamps that hung from the high ceiling had a Moorish look about them, and the massive furniture was carved from woods that were meant to last down the centuries, kept polished with the beeswax she could smell so that it had the gleam of chased metal. Deep were the cupboards, large enough for a child to get lost in, with shadowy corners for games of hide-and-seek.

Had the cousins played in these cupboards when they were boys in this house? Destine fingered the old-fashioned pots and jars on the dressing-table, and saw her own image reflected in the shield-shaped mirror. She was startled by how pale she looked, standing here like a ghost in this Spanish room, her silvery hair making her eyes seem darker than they were.

This had been the house of the man who had killed Matt, and it was incredible that she should be here. What quirk of destiny had designed it so? What devil had whispered in the ear of her godmother to make that usually kind woman suggest that she come here?

A tremor of sheer nerves ran through Destine's slender body. Even the contours and features of her own face seemed strange to her, and she walked from the mirror to the bed, across the carpets of Moroccan design, in which the colours mingled as naturally as dyes dropped into a blue ocean. She paused beside the bed and saw the four figures carved upon the bedposts . . . an angel and a knight at either side of the headrest, a dragon and a demon at the foot.

Protection for the sleeper, even as danger advanced from the shadows.

Destine backed away from the bed . . . no, she couldn't sleep here! She would sit in that woven-cane armchair placed near the windows, and wait for the morning to come. With the first light she would leave, for Don Cicatrice would be only too glad to drive her away from the *casa*. Though he hadn't known that she was the widow of Matthew Mitchell, he had from the moment of meeting her been dubious of her suitability as his cousin Cosima's nurse.

On legs that felt tired and shaky Destine approached the cane armchair and sat down upon the cushioned seat; after a moment or two she allowed her head to sink back against the cushioned headrest. God, she had not felt this exhausted since those early days of her widowhood, and being a nurse she knew it to be an exhaustion of the emotions that drained all the vitality from the body. She also knew that she needed to sleep, but she obstinately refused to sleep in that great bed, which would be so shadowy, so isolated when the lamps were out and the netting was pulled. She would have nightmares if she slept there, and it would come as no change for her to doze in a chair. She had done that often enough when on night duty.

The moths buzzed about the lamps, and she could smell the smoke of the oil mingling with that aroma of beeswax mixed with thyme, in which the bed linen was probably stored. Her heavy eyelids drifted downwards and all sensation became dulled as sleep took slow possession of her mind and her body. Her fingers relaxed their hold upon the arms of the chair and her arms fell lax at the sides. Her head fell sideways against the cushion and her silvery hair lay like a ruffled wing across her face. Her lips relaxed from the taut lines into which they had been drawn for the past hour, and in sleep all the youth returned to her rather lovely face ... she was totally unaware of the moment when someone tapped upon the door of the bedroom, with its white walls that took the shadows and made them seem alive. With its crucifix carved from silvery wood, and its big bed guarded and threatened by all the opposing elements in human nature.

The journey and the shock of finding herself among the very people she would have gone a thousand miles to avoid had taken their toll and Destine was fast asleep when the bedroom door opened and dark eyes dwelt upon her in the cane chair.

The man had walked silently even on the tiles of the courtyard, so he made no sound at all as he crossed the room with the oriental carpets underfoot. He stood looking down at her, but Destine slept on, and was to remain lost in the

26

realms of sleep until the morning sunlight stabbed through the oval, stained-glass window above the silvery-wood cross and sent spirals of colour in a rainbow across the room.

Destine's eyes blinked open as those winking colours played against her eyelids. She lay still for several moments, gazing at the window and the cross and wondering where on earth she was. She had slept so deeply that the return to awareness was a slow one . . . and then it all rushed back and she gave a gasp and sat up, finding herself not in the cane chair but on the bed, wrapped in the quilt, with her shoes removed.

But . . . but how had it come about that she was here, on the bed, when she remembered distinctly that she had settled down for the night in that chair over by the windows where the curtains were still drawn? Had she been so tired that she hadn't realised that she had crawled on to the bed after all? Kicked off her shoes and rolled herself in the quilt against the cold that had crept into the room?

It wasn't cold now. The ray of sunlight that touched her hand was warm, and that very warmth told her that she had slept longer than she had meant to. She had resolved last night to be gone from this house at the crack of dawn, and she glanced swiftly at her wristwatch to see the exact time, only to find that not having been wound the little watch had stopped in the night. Such strong sunlight meant that it was now about seven or eight o'clock, and Destine untangled herself from the white quilt and was about to put her feet to the floor when a sudden tap at the door froze her into stillness.

She was staring at the door, her eyes strangely apprehensive in the tousled frame of her hair, when the handle turned and the door swung open. A woman stood there, staring fixedly at Destine. Then she came a little farther into the room and the heavy silk of her robe rustled about her thin and elegant figure. Her hair was covered by a lace

27

sleeping-cap, but there was nothing very sleepy about the eyes that raked over Destine, taking in the fact that she had slept in her clothes, and had lain on the bed rather than in it.

'You arrived late,' the woman said, and she spoke English with an attractive, slightly broken accent, 'so we didn't meet last night. You are Nurse Chard, are you not?'

'Yes.' The word came out huskily and Destine swallowed to relieve the dryness of her throat. She assessed the visitor to her room as a woman in her late fifties; still rather beautiful, with that beauty rooted in good bone structure rather than in frequent visits to the cosmetic parlours. Her eyes were magnificent . . . dark as jet and with a touch of the orient in the way they were shaped. Her skin was pale as ivory and almost unlined; what gave her away as a woman approaching sixty was the veining of the hands and the drawn cords of the neck.

It came as no real surprise to Destine when the woman said: 'I am the Marquesa, and as we didn't meet last night I came to bid you welcome to the *casa*. You must have been extremely tired after your journey, Nurse, to have fallen asleep just as you were. I hope my nephew made you welcome? I hope, also, that you weren't—ah, but you are a nurse and you have seen disfigured faces quite often. It wouldn't bother you, to be met so late by a man so scarred, eh?'

'No—' Destine shook her head, and the realisation struck sharply that she was going to have to tell this gracious woman that she had no intention of remaining at the *casa*, and that woman was going to think her a fool who was frightened by her nephew's face. The real truth was far harsher . . . how could she blurt it out, that she was the widow of the man whom this woman's son had killed with his reckless driving? A mother loves her son, devil or saint. A mother reveres his memory, good or bad.

'What is it, Nurse?' The Marquesa looked rather concerned as she came towards the bed. 'Are you sick?'

'No, Señora Marquesa, I'm perfectly all right.' Destine slid from the bed and sought her shoes, and as she put them on grappled wildly with the problem of telling the Marquesa that she couldn't stay here; that she could not take on the task of caring for her invalid daughter. It was the fault of the nephew that she was in this predicament. He could have woken her an hour ago and driven her to the station before his aunt was aware of her presence here. He could have said that she had not arrived after all, for no one but he had seen her last night. None of the servants had been about at that late hour, and though he had asked her if she wanted coffee she had said no. There would have been no evidence of her arrival and her departure had he aroused her before the other members of the household were awake. She would have straightened the bedcovers and left the room as pristine as it had been last night.

Now it was too late for that . . . now she had to make some improbable excuse about not remaining here.

'I can see that something is wrong.' The Marquesa came quite close to Destine and studied her face. 'Are you not happy to work here, Nurse Chard? Are you afraid that we are too isolated – ?'

'Yes, I am afraid of that.' Destine caught swiftly at this lifeline. 'I had no idea that the *casa* was so far from the village and places of entertainment. I don't think it would be any use my staying here – I had better leave right away –'

'Without even a meeting with my daughter?' The Marquesa looked faintly quizzical. 'You don't seem to me to be a frivolous young woman who needs constant entertainment – I suspect that something else is troubling you. Was my nephew in any way – discouraging? He was not enthusiastic when it was suggested that I employ an English nurse, and he is not a man to conceal a truth with a sweet lie. What has he done? Told you that you are the wrong type of

29

person for the position of nurse to my beloved Cosima?'

Destine hesitated, and then inclined her head. 'Perhaps your nephew is right, Señora Marquesa. It seems hardly worthwhile my starting the job only to conclude it in a matter of days—'

'Do you usually give in so easily?' The Marquesa wore a slight smile. 'I know that my nephew can be an intimidating man, but you don't strike me as a young woman easily cowed down by a man, no matter how forceful his personality, or how sinister his face may suppose him to be. Surely, having made such a long journey, you won't permit it to be a fruitless one? I am inclined to like the look of you, Nurse Chard. You have good bones and a look of courage. Please do stay! Give yourself a chance to like us—I shall understand if, in about a week, you decide that you have made a mistake in coming to Xanas.'

Destine knew that she should have been decisive and ignored the appeal and the charm of this woman who had not become bitter under the blow of losing her son and seeing her daughter crippled. But she hesitated, and in that instant the Marquesa used the pushbell on the table beside the bed.

'You must have coffee—or tea if you would prefer. And breakfast. Our *ama de llaves* will take excellent care of you. She is named Victoria, and her slightly gruff manner conceals a good heart. I shall see you later, Nurse. *Hasta luego.*'

The bedroom door closed behind the robed figure and Destine was left with the feeling that all decision had been firmly but graciously taken from her, and that she was going to have to stay at the *casa* a while longer, whether she liked it or not. Biting her lip, and feeling as if she had been disarmed into cowardice, she walked to the windows and drew back the drapes to let in the full glory of the southern sunlight.

It flooded in through the curves and loops and intricate

30

weavings of the lace cage that completely enclosed the balcony of the connecting windows, making a fairly deep enclosure where cane chairs and a circular table were arranged. In earthenware pots were small orange trees hung with yellow fruit, the fiery dance of fuchsias, and a hibiscus with dark shining leaves. In and out of the ornamental iron itself there curled a vine that dripped with honey-coloured bells in which the bees were already humming.

Destine was again caught by unexpected charm – it was a dalliance balcony, where a woman might dally with a book or a letter or a piece of embroidery, and not be disturbed by the outside world, though it would be there for her to see and hear, and breathe. What was that perfume? Destine took a deep breath and realised that it was tobacco, sweet and strong on the warm air.

Were there plantations of tobacco as well as sugar cane? Don Cicatrice had said of the region that it was almost tropical, where many exotic things grew.

Destine stood upon the balcony and saw the glint of water courses running through the patios and gardens of the *casa*. Beside them, shading the many flowering shrubs, were palm trees with thick girths towering upwards into a vast crest of pendulous leaves. She caught the flash of multi-coloured wings and heard the singing of many birds; she also heard the cicadas . . . voice of the sun, insistent and in total unison, issuing in a mysterious fashion from every corner of the estate, from tiny creatures never visible.

So absorbed was she in the low throbbing sound that Destine wasn't aware when the *ama de llaves* (mistress of the keys) entered the room. It was the rattling of the keys on a chain that recalled her from the garden sounds to the bedroom, and she turned swiftly to see a figure straight out of a drama about the Victorians, clad entirely in black, the chain of household keys looped about the waist of her dress. The woman's face was brown as a nut and equally wrinkled, and

31

her dark gaze was penetrating as she came toward Destine.

'I will take your orders for breakfast, *señora,*' she said. 'And answer any questions you may have. You will understand that I am a busy person, so please to tell me how you prefer your breakfast in the mornings. Tea or coffee will be available, for this is a civilized house, despite the accusations of the previous nurses that we live at the back of beyond and have no television set on which to watch the Saga of the Forsythians.'

It was to Destine's credit that she kept a straight face, though she longed to smile at the housekeeper's remark. The woman was a character, and only here in the southern region of Spain, where a number of things still related to the past, was it possible to meet her sort.

Destine came in from the balcony, and at once she was made conscious of her slept-in appearance as the sharp eyes probed her from head to foot.

'I should like a pot of English tea, if you will be so kind. Did the previous nurse eat up here, or down in the kitchen? And do tell me where the bathroom is situated.'

'You may have breakfast here in your room, *señora,* though it saves the legs of my staff if you eat downstairs. Not in the kitchen for you are not a member of the staff, but in the morning *sala* or out on one of the patios. And now if you will come with me I will show you the bathroom which is fairly convenient to this room.'

'Thank you.' Destine followed the rustle of bombazine and the rattle of keys along the gallery, which led in one direction to the staircase, and in the other to a range of doors heavily carved like the door of her own room.

They walked past these doors until the *ama de llaves* paused at the very end of the gallery. 'This is the room of the bath, the shower, and the toilet, *señora.* You will find that the supply of water varies with the amount required by the *dueño* for the watering of the plantations. Water is precious to us in this region and is pumped down at some expense from the mountains. It is a strange colour at times, but quite wholesome to use.'

'Is it warm?' Destine wanted to know.

Victoria shrugged her black-clad shoulders. 'Sometimes yes, sometimes no. You will have to learn to take it as it comes, *señora*. It is well understood that your own country has all the modern amenities, but when we run out of gasolene to pump the generators my son Escamillo has to drive many miles in order to buy more. Nurses! They think they should be treated like visiting nobility!'

This time Destine couldn't suppress a smile. 'I do assure you that I don't expect any special sort of treatment,' she said. 'The *casa* seems to me a most attractive and well-run establishment. You spoke of a *dueño*, but I understood that the Marquesa was a widow, and that her only son had died in the bullring.'

It cost an effort for Destine to say this so calmly, but if she was going to remain here at the House of the Grilles, then she was going to have to associate herself with all those details which her godmother had withheld from her.

'The husband of the Marquesa died a long time ago, and it is very true that her only son is lost to her. But you have met the *dueño*. It was he who fetched you to the *casa*, though it should have been Escamillo who came for you. My son had been away on an errand all that day, so Don Cicatrice drove down to the station, not using the car, for it was a spare part that my son had to go for and the nearest garage is some miles away. We are very isolated.'

Victoria added this rather dourly, as if she knew in advance that it would cause yet another nurse to make her departure before long. It would not be isolation, as Destine knew. Somehow it didn't worry her to be in the heart of the country ... it only worried her to be in the heart of this family.

33

'So he is the master,' she murmured. 'The man in command?'

'Don Cicatrice has run the estate for the Señora Marquesa for many years.' Victoria gave Destine a sharp look, as if she would brook no whisper against that man with the scarred face. 'Her son was uninterested in the plantations, though not in the money that they provide. He had the looks and the charm, that one, but it is the *dueño* who is the man. It doesn't concern him to conquer women or bulls. He is *solterón*, and no one will change him.'

A crusted bachelor, in other words. Set in his ways, and probably aware that his face was unlikely to inspire romantic feelings in women.

A mental image of his scarred face flickered in and out of Destine's mind. In the half-light of the hall last night he had borne a sinister resemblance to the dead Manolito, and Destine felt a stirring of curiosity about how he would strike her when she saw him by daylight.

'So he is the *dueño*?' she murmured.

'And why not?' demanded Victoria. 'Who has a better right? If that foolish Cosima had had any sense she would have married him.'

'But they're cousins,' Destine exclaimed.

'So? Don't cousins marry in your country, *señora*? Here in Xanas it frequently happens, and none the worse for that. If there are good traits in a family, then they are doubled by such a marriage.'

'And what if there are bad traits?' Destine asked. 'They, too, would be doubled – perhaps that is why these two cousins hesitated. After all, Cosima's brother was no saint – more of a satyr.'

Victoria stared with sharp eyes at Destine. 'Whatever the skeletons in the closets of this family, they are none of your concern, Nurse. It is merely your place to take care of Cosima, and if you have listened to gossip about her brother,

34

then I should keep it to yourself. She was very fond of him. It came as a great shock when he was killed and did her no good at all. What with that – what with everything else!' The *ama de llaves* threw up her hands with a very Spanish imprecation, and it was obvious from the way she spoke about the members of this family that she had been part of the household for many years.

'Life can be unfair to some,' she muttered. 'Often to those least deserving of it.'

'I know,' said Destine, from her heart. Matt had been but twenty-six when that great car had slammed into him and hurled him through the windscreen of his own car. In her nightmares she still saw what she had loved turned from a living man into a dead and faceless shape. She shuddered, and then reached out to take hold of the handle of the bathroom door.

'Will it be all right if I have my breakfast in my room, just for today?' she asked.

Victoria shrugged her black-clad shoulders. 'Very well,' she said. 'So you wish for tea, bacon and eggs?'

'Please.'

'It will be ready in half an hour.' Abruptly the housekeeper touched Destine on the arm. 'I was told you are a widow?'

'Yes.' Destine's fingers gripped the handle until her knuckles whitened. 'My husband died two years ago.'

'You are young to be a widow,' said Victoria, and with a rustle of bombazine and a rattling of keys she went off along the corridor in the direction of the stairs. Destine entered the old-fashioned but commodious bathroom, and she realised that she had committed herself to at least a week in this house. She didn't want to stay, but something was holding her here; curiosity, perhaps, for it certainly wasn't sympathy. How could she feel anything but hatred for any member of Manolito's family? His blood was theirs. His sins might also

35

be theirs. Instinctively she knew that she ought to go, but when she bent over the bath to turn on the hot-water tap she froze and was aware of nothing but the enormous, long-legged spider that crouched at the bottom of the tub, black as sin against the white porcelain.

Ordinarily Destine was unafraid of what crept and crawled, having worked in hospitals too long for her nerves to be shaken by such things, but since last night her nerves had been on a knife edge and before she could stop herself she had let out a yell.

Almost instantly the door was thrust open behind her and when she turned to look she found herself confronted by a tall figure with water-tousled hair, a bare brown chest, and the rest of him belted into tight black trousers. For an instant her gaze was fixed upon the disc of gold that gleamed against his coppery skin, the chain on which it hung buried in the tangle of dark hair that rose almost to his throat. The taut skin across his shoulders had that burnished look of a body not long from under a cold shower, and for some reason Destine's breath caught in her throat.

She was a nurse, and a widow, but never before had she been made so aware of the animal vitality of a male body. She saw the muscles ripple under the taut skin as their owner stepped further into the bathroom.

'What's the matter?' he demanded. 'Why did you cry out?'

She remembered the spider and suddenly felt as foolish as a schoolgirl. She gestured towards the bottom of the bath, for there was nothing else she could do.

His gaze followed the direction of her fingers, and she didn't dare to meet his eyes when they swivelled to her face. 'And that's why you screamed?' His tone of voice was utterly sardonic. 'I thought at least that a snake had crawled in.'

'You would,' she rejoined. 'The thing took me by surprise,

36

that's all. I'm not normally an hysterical fool, and you must admit that it's rather larger than the variety we have in England.'

'Perhaps,' he drawled, and bending over the bath he lifted the spider in the palm of his hand and carried it to the window. He tossed it out, and then turned to look steadily at Destine. She looked back at him and suppressed the shiver that ran through her as she saw the sun reflected on his face. It wasn't his scar alone that made her feel like screaming again – it was the look he had of Manolito de Obregon. Tall like he was, supple as fine steel, almost black-eyed; eyes in which the night could lose itself.

'I understand that you have seen the Marquesa,' he said, and his voice had a sudden edge to it. 'She has asked you to stay, eh?'

'Yes.' Destine had to look away from him, and instantly, in a single stride, he was across the bathroom and she gasped as he gripped her chin with his fingers and forced her face upwards, so that she had to look at him whether she liked it or not.

'If you stay, Nurse Chard, each day you will see this face of mine. It makes you shudder, eh? Makes you want to turn away? Well, the choice is yours – I can drive you to the station right now and you need never see me again. Last night you begged me to do that.'

'I know,' she said. 'I want to go and yet – yet I feel I should stay, for a while. It isn't only that I have a duty as a nurse, but – '

'But you're curious about a family that seems to have a direct bearing on your own unhappiness. You want the answer to why your husband had to die, and you think you might find it here. Am I right?'

'Perhaps.' She blinked her lashes in an attempt to avoid his eyes; never in her life had she seen eyes so impenetrably dark, so that to look into them was like losing herself. 'I don't know—it's all so mixed up, and if I run away I might hate myself for a coward.'

'Instead you are going to stay and hate me?' There was a dry note in his voice, and his fingers gripped her chin a little tighter so that her gaze was fixed upon his face. 'Take a good look at me in the daylight, Nurse Chard. Last night you said a strange thing, that I was Manolito resurrected for you—it could almost be true, for when they carried him from that bullring at Seville his handsome face had been ripped open and had he lived—but he didn't. He paid his price, as we all must. Go away, Nurse! Go back to your England and try to forget—'

'Forget!' She looked at him with blazing blue eyes. 'You could never have loved anyone, if you think it's so easy to forget—a smile, a way of talking together, a sense of belonging. What are you? A man of iron?'

'Then stay!' He said it harshly and let go of her so abruptly that she felt unbalanced and fell back against the wall and knocked her shoulder. She winced, but his face remained implacable. 'There is a saying, *señora*, that if you choose to reside with dragons then you must prepare yourself to be burned. I shall see you later, no doubt.

He strode to the door and with a brief inclination of his dark head was gone, leaving Destine to nurse her shoulder. All the hate that had accumulated in her heart in the past two years was now directed at him; it had to find an outlet and now it had found one. Her eyes burned with all that pent-up hatred . . . she was in no doubt that this cousin of Manolito de Obregon was the same arrogant type, going his own way without a care for anyone in his path. So sure of the strength of his own body . . . so certain that his heart could never be touched.

Destine swung to the mirror that was attached to the bathroom wall and she stared for a long time at her own face. With a strange sense of detachment she saw again what Matt

38

had seen when he was alive, the eyes that were a true blue without a hint of grey or green in them. The hair that was like silver-gilt, framing the good skin and the shapely features of her face.

With that face, and that slim body, she would like to punish the arrogant cousin who was so alike to Manolito de Obregon. Such men thought themselves immune from feelings of love. They thought of it as an emotion for weak fools . . . how she would like to prove that arrogance could be brought to its knees by what it sneered at.

Forget! He had said it as he might say any casual thing. Forget that Matt was killed on their wedding day, all his hopes and desires ended in a moment, even as the sun shone and a tiny bell of confetti fell from Destine's sleeve as she ran to rejoin him, clutching the handbag that for a fateful moment in time had taken her away from him.

Destine's eyes reflected in the mirror were as hard as gems in that moment. She would like to teach Don Cicatrice what it felt like to love someone, and then lose them. She would like to take his heart, and break it.

When she returned to her room after her bath she found that a tray of bacon and eggs, and a pot of tea, had been placed on the balcony table. The floor-length windows stood open and the sunlight was flooding in over the oriental patterns of the carpets. The bed had been straightened, and her suitcase stood on a stool waiting to be unpacked.

Well, she couldn't spend today in the rumpled trouser-suit in which she had slept . . . again she glanced at the bed and wondered why it was that she couldn't remember leaving the cane chair last night to clamber on the bed. Was it possible that she had been put there? Had those hard coppery arms of Don Cicatrice lifted her and carried her to the bed while she was deeply asleep?

He would find her weight no problem, and that he was as complex as hell she didn't doubt for one moment. It would never be the emotion of kindness that motivated any of his actions; if he had come to this room last night and seen her asleep in the chair he would merely have thought it the sensible thing to place her on the bed. God, how silently he must move, how adroit must be his movements if he could carry her from the chair to the bed and not disturb her. Had he, in his irony, thought that if he woke her she might be scared by his face?

Destine unlocked her suitcase and began to search for fresh clothes. Yes, she had a choice, she could stay or she could leave. 'Will they expect me to wear a uniform?' she had asked her godmother. The Condesa had smiled and shaken her head. 'These people are not conventional,' she had replied. 'You will be surprised by them.'

Surprised was hardly the appropriate word. Destine shook out a dark blue dress trimmed with white, of a material that didn't crease, and a few minutes later she was wearing it and had combed her hair into a smooth chignon that left the line of her temples, jaw and throat looking clear and uncluttered, and yet not severe.

She ate her breakfast in the sunlight, and had just finished off with a tangerine when the young maid came to collect the tray. The girl had evidently been told that the English *tata* spoke good Spanish, for she made no attempt to speak any English and told Destine in a swift flow of words that the Marquesa would like to see her if she was now quite ready, so that she could meet the Señora Cosima.

Destine followed the girl, nerves braced for her first encounter with the young woman who had no idea that her brother had caused as much havoc to Destine's life as the attack of polio had caused to hers. They went down the curving flight of stairs to the arcaded hall, where from the cool white cloisters a tall figure suddenly appeared in their path.

'Go along to the kitchen, Pepita,' he said. 'I wish to have

a few words with the nurse, and then I will take her to Tia Felicitas.'

The girl cast a rather frightened look at him, Destine noticed, and then with a bob and a rush she was gone, and he gave a brief sardonic laugh. 'Each time we break in a new maid—these girls will marry as soon as they possibly can—she brings with her a dozen superstitions regarding myself. Did you know that when Lucifero fell from grace and was hurled from heaven, he struck his face and was henceforth marked? Well, it's one of the many colourful yarns that country people spin, and girls will be girls—will they not, Nurse Chard?'

As he spoke he lounged against one of the tiled pillars that supported the arcade, and there was something more disturbing about him than Destine cared to admit to herself. He wore a white shirt that made his skin seem Arab-dark, and that look of indolent strength was more flagrant by daylight than it had been in the darkness. He wore the night like a mask, but now she saw him revealed as a man in his early thirties, with not a hint of sympathy or tenderness in that satanically marked face.

'What do you want, *señor?*' she asked. 'I don't like to keep your aunt waiting.'

'All I want is your assurance that you won't say things to upset Tia Felicitas. If you are going to stay here, then you promise me that you will say nothing about your husband having died because of Manolito. It would be too cruel to a woman who has suffered—'

'Don't you think I've suffered?' Destine asked quietly.

'You are young,' he said, and his eyes were quite unrelenting as they took in her slender figure in the dark blue dress piped with white around the collar, the piping extending down the front of the dress to the hem. 'And I'm sure you know that you are attractive, and your life can begin again. But the Marquesa must live on her memories, and grief has softened those and I don't want them made harsh for her. If you hurt that woman in any way—' He took a step towards Destine and automatically she backed away from him, seeing his lips curl as he took her retreat for the usual feminine reaction to his scar. 'I think you and I understand each other, don't we?'

It was her turn to look him up and down, and she did so deliberately. 'You have judged me, *señor,* and now I will judge you. You have taken me for a widow on the lookout for a rich protector—am I supposed to mistake you for the *muy rico hombre?*'

'It might be a mistake if you took me for the usual fool, likely to be dazzled by your hair and your blue eyes,' he drawled.

'Why should I want to dazzle you?' she asked. 'I should imagine it would be like trying to strike a match against a piece of steel.'

'So long as you know,' he said, a curl to his lips. 'I shouldn't wish you to dwell under the delusion that you can make blue eyes at me and imagine I shall take it for anything more than hate, or pity.'

She stared at him, and felt a strange stab at the heart. 'I can't imagine any woman feeling pity for you, *señor,*' she said. 'The idea is fantastic!'

'Is it equally fantastic that any woman should love me?' he queried, and again he took a step in her direction, and before she knew it, she was backed into an angle of one of the arcades, the curves at either side of her, and he in front of her, tall, mocking, careless of anyone's feelings towards him, whether it be hate or love.

'Women aren't put off by scars,' she said, looking up at him with defiance in her vivid blue eyes. 'They're only skin deep—it's what is inside a man that matters. You exaggerate all reaction to your face—you use it as a weapon to keep people at bay. You don't like people, do you?'

'Were you trained to nurse the mind as well as the body?' he asked drily. 'You presume to know a lot about me on such short acquaintance.'

'You presume the same,' she rejoined.

'Why?' His dark eyes ran over her hair and dwelt on the streak of sheer silver that ran through it. 'Is the needle still pricking because I said that your hair was dyed? For that I apologise, but after seeing so many peroxide blondes on the beaches of Spain I presumed that a real blonde would be as rare as the smile on the face of the Mona Lisa.'

'It isn't only English women who like Spanish beaches, *señor,*' she said stiffly.

'Maybe not.' He shrugged his shoulders as if he had little time to spare for any of the European women who came to Spain for their summer tan. 'I really couldn't care less, except to say that many of them are an eyesore in their skimpy bathing suits over bulging bottoms and breasts. But that is beside the point—I must exact from you a promise that you will be discreet about the part my cousin played in your life. If I can't have that promise, then you must go, Nurse Chard.'

'You speak as if you have the authority to drive me out,' she said. 'Surely this is the Marquesa's home?'

'Yes, but I am in charge of the running of it.'

'Head cook and bottle washer,' Destine couldn't help saying. 'The *dueño* who cracks the whip.'

'Exactly,' he drawled. 'Again we understand each other. My aunt has enough to concern her without the worry of minor things, such as the employment of staff. As I told you last night, I was against an English nurse being hired, but it is true that Cosima has not shown much improvement in the hands of the nurses she has so far had. It is all in the mind, of course. She's unbearably unhappy and so it affects her physical condition. If you can do anything to help Cosima, then it will be a small miracle. You may try, Nurse Chard, if you make me that promise.'

'Did you really imagine, *señor*, that I was going to dash into your aunt's presence, crying out that her son killed my husband?' Destine stood there against the white stone, defiant of him, and yet made strangely nervous by the lithe, ruthless strength of his body, and the cynical contempt he seemed to have for women who weren't Latin. She had heard of the way European women cheapened themselves with Spaniards, almost unaware that the dash of the Moor in these men made the crude flaunting of the body almost a sign that any woman who did it was little better than a woman who sold herself.

Colour stung her cheeks . . . there was something about him, a hard pride and self-sufficiency that made her feel cheap for having thought that she could use her looks to make a fool of him. Her eyes skimmed that fearful scar that had been inflicted when he was a teenager.

'A woman out for vengeance is as dangerous as a woman scorned,' he said. 'Last night you couldn't wait to leave the *casa*. This morning you decide to stay. It would hardly be unnatural that I wonder about your change of mind. What is on your mind, Nurse Chard? Some form of revenge against Manolito's family?'

'No!' But she said it too sharply, too defiantly, and instantly his eyes narrowed until they had a cruel, glittering-look. His hand reached out and closed on her shoulder, and she felt the pressure of his fingers all the way through her.

'No,' she said again. 'What a thing to suggest—I'm not like that!'

'Aren't you?' He stared down into her eyes. 'You're a woman, and only a fool would ever presume to know all that goes on in a woman's mind. It twists and turns like a serpent in the garden itself, and it's been that way since Adam fell a victim to feminine wiles. Be careful, Nurse. I am on to you, and I wouldn't hesitate to break your white neck if you did anything to hurt the Marquesa. She has had her share of

44

pain, and she means more to me than any lily-white creature like you – you're little more than a girl, and you have had no taste, yet, of real passion. You see, you flinch from the word! Everything is permissive where you come from – everything but the passion that springs from a total giving. You take from the moment you are born, but you never give. Yours is an acquisitive society tinged with malice . . . so what is it that suddenly makes it bearable for you to stay here, *señora*?'

She stared back at him and just couldn't find the words to explain with. Was he right . . . was it sheer malice that made her want to stay in this house with these people who had been Manolito de Obregon's closest relatives?

'Well, Nurse?' His fingers slid deliberately around her slim neck, pressing against her skin so that she felt the hard tips of his hand, and the masculine warmth that seemed to penetrate to her blood. 'Has your tongue suddenly lost itself?'

'Do you always know what motivates your actions?' she asked him. 'Are you that sure of yourself, *señor*?'

'No.' He shook his head and his glinting eyes dwelt on her lips, only lightly coloured, curving against her pale skin. 'You lost your husband on your wedding day, eh?'

'Yes – ' She shuddered at the memory . . . at the touch of Manolito's cousin.

'Then can you wonder that I ask if you bear malice towards us?' Still he spoke in that unpitying voice. 'It would not be surprising if you did.'

'Perhaps you are afraid to let me stay,' she said.

'Afraid – for myself?' He gave a scoffing smile and swept his eyes up and down her body. 'Do you plan to take on the role of Delilah? May I say that you are hardly built for it.'

'I – I shouldn't want to seduce you,' she gasped, denying what had crossed her mind, and seeing in his eyes a cynical, masculine awareness that made her feel gauche, and at a dis-

45

advantage. She tried to break free of him, and instantly, with a reflex that was animal in its swiftness, his other arm curled around her and he brought her painfully close to his hard warmth of body; the torso bare and brown under the white shirt, legs long and muscled in the black trousers that fitted close like a skin.

Her blue eyes warred with his dark ones ... his strength was absolute, but Destine hadn't known until now that she could feel so shockingly weak in a man's arms. It had never happened before and she panicked. 'Let me go!' And when a smile curled against his mouth she struck out at him and her hand found his scar instead of the smile, and that seemed to infuriate him.

'You don't like my face, eh?' He thrust it down at her. 'Then find out what it's like to have my face this close to you!'

She felt the warm rush of his breath, and then she felt the crush of his lips ... she had not been kissed for two years, but this kiss from an angry Spaniard brought back no memories of Matt's tenderness. It was like a flame burning across the barren years ... it scorched and destroyed the tender yearnings, and all Destine was aware of was a merciless body locked against hers, and a mouth that didn't care how much it hurt her.

Her release when it came was cruelly abrupt ... she tried to steady herself but swayed into the hard curve of the arcade. 'Y-you're a devil,' she whispered, 'like he was!'

'You refer to Manolito?' He regarded her intently, hands thrusting into the pockets of his trousers.

'Yes!' She flung back her head and hated him with her eyes. 'That's the mark of the devil on your face, though I shouldn't think you've ever been close enough to heaven to have been thrown out of it!'

His lips twisted when she said that. 'How clever of you to

guess,' he said. 'You will want to leave now, eh? I will go and tell Escamillo to get out the conveyance – '

'No,' she broke in. 'I'm not running away from you! That's what you'd like, to see me scuttle away like a scared rabbit just because you – kissed me. I'm staying, whether you like it or not!'

'I don't like it,' he said deliberately. 'But if you are staying, then I would advise you to sleep in the bed that is provided for you, and not in a chair. This is an almost tropical region, as I told you, and the occasional mosquito flies in – you would not enjoy its bite. The bed netting will protect that inviting white skin of yours.'

'Was it you – ' Destine bit her lip, while a little colour flared across her cheekbones. 'Last night that bed seemed so enormous and had such strange carvings on it. I – I didn't think about the possible advent of a mosquito.'

'Or a man?' he drawled. 'It would be droll, would it not, if we had to nurse you out of a fever?'

She glanced swiftly from his mocking eyes, and tilted her chin to let him know that she wouldn't want his attentions in any capacity, though she didn't doubt that he could take arrogant command of any emergency.

'Aren't you going to thank me for transferring you from the chair to the greater comfort of the bed?' he asked, looking sardonic.

'Thanks,' she said briefly, and wished to heaven that it were possible to forget the helpless feeling that had swept over her during those conscious moments in his arms. Last night she had not been aware of those arms with their muscles that rippled like fine steel under the warm, sun-coppered skin. 'And now will you take me to the Marquesa, *señor*?'

'By all means, Nurse.' He walked with his silent tread as he escorted her across the hall, and bowed her into the *sala*, and she caught the mocking gleam in his eyes a moment before he turned away and left her standing there. She strove

47

not to glance after him, but couldn't help herself. He was unusually tall for a Spaniard . . . an unusual man in several respects, who might brush off most women as if they were moths that bothered him.

CHAPTER THREE

THAT encounter with Don Cicatrice had not helped to compose Destine, and in a desperate bid to regain her self-control she took a quick look around the *sala* and saw at once that nothing here had been replaced by modern items of luxury.

The *sala* had that beautiful, gracious air of a room in which the furniture was old but cared for, standing upon carpets dimmed by the years but speckless, and shaded from the full sun by long drapes that harboured not a hint of dust. This was not a family of new riches, but one as long established as this region in the south, where long years ago the Moors had ruled and set their mark.

Her eyes dwelt upon the two Goya paintings set side by side on the wall, one of a woman in carnation red, the other of a matador in black and silver. The flesh tones were superb, the eyes bold and black, the colours touchable.

'You are fond of paintings, Nurse Chard?' The Marquesa came lightly across the carpets towards Destine. 'Goya was a master of his art, was he not?'

'I thought they must be originals.' Destine looked, then, at the woman who was so unbelievably the mother of Manolito. She wore a fine linen suit in an ivory colour, with beneath it a dark silk blouse. Her hair was a shining white and perfectly arranged, and a certain curiosity dwelt in her eyes as she studied her daughter's new nurse.

'You are a very personable young woman,' she said, 'and I wonder why you left London to come here. If you were a plain and efficient-looking nurse then I might be less inquisitive. But somehow you seem too feminine to be entirely the career-minded type – liberated, is that not how they say it? In her letter the Condesa de Calva intimated that you had no special circle of friends and kept very much to yourself and devoted your time to your work. I therefore expected someone—well, far less attractive and smart.'

'I'm sorry if my godmother misled you, Señora Marquesa,' Destine spoke politely, and thought to herself that *she* was the one who had been misled. 'Since I lost my husband I have lacked interest in anything but my work, and I don't intend to marry again.'

'If a woman of my age said such a thing, then it would be understandable—please to sit down.' The Marquesa directed a hand towards one of the tawny-gold sofas. 'This is not an interview, but a friendly chat between two people who have in common the care of my daughter. I don't wish to act as an employer and I am hoping, Nurse, that you don't wish to be merely the efficient supervisor of Cosima's comfort? Do you? My main wish when I decided to take the Condesa's advice and employ an English nurse was that you might become a friend to Cosima. You are a young and pretty widow. You know what it feels like to lose what you love. You have that in common with her, and I hoped that you might become her *confidante,* for she needs one very badly, and she might learn to speak with more ease to a young woman of her own age, who is obviously cultured and intelligent. What do you say—Destine? That is your first name, is it not? An unusual, almost significant name. It might have been destiny that arranged for you to come to us.'

Destine sat tensely on the edge of the sofa, facing the twin sofa on which the Marquesa sat. The other woman smiled and leaned forward, placing a hand lightly on Destine's knee. 'You seem so unrelaxed—don't you feel that you are going to be happy with us? Are you now feeling sorry that you left London to come to Xanas? Why did you when you seem so uncertain of what you have done?'

'I—I felt I needed a change.' Destine strove to be more at

ease, for she liked the Marquesa and felt that Don Cicatrice couldn't be right when he said that the wish to bear malice was her motivation in remaining here at the *casa*. He couldn't be right, could he? Destine was uncertain and it showed.

'A change is always good, and no doubt you have felt much saddened at being widowed so young. You could have had no chance of any real happiness—' The Marquesa sighed and glanced at the heavy ruby and diamond ring on her hand. 'In a way, however, I could almost have wished that Cosima was widowed instead of merely separated from a man whom she remains hopeful of being with again. How she can still love him is a mystery—but love is a mystery, I suppose. It comes like a sharp arrow striking, bringing pain or pleasure, or both at the same time. Who can really be armoured against it, and Cosima was always a vulnerable sort of girl, which makes it doubly worse for her to have been physically hurt by the polio, and mentally hurt by her husband's defection at a time when she needed him so desperately.'

The Marquesa leaned back in her seat and her lovely dark eyes brooded on the Goya painting of the matador. 'A year ago I lost my son, Destine, so you will understand that Cosima is doubly precious to me. I tell you frankly that I always hoped she would marry her cousin, but young girls will be swayed by a handsome face and when this other man came into her life I had my doubts about him, but I was persuaded by her passion for him that she would be happy. I should have been cruel. I should have denied him to her, for she was young for her age, and I had some control over her having been mother and father to her all these years— you may not know it, but my husband was killed at Estremadura where we once had a large *finca* where horses were bred. The boys were both there, my son with his cousin, both of them being of a similar age. It was a great tragedy! There

51

was a fire in the stables – I thought I should go quite insane, and it was only the intensive care that had to be given Artez – in those days he was always Artez and it was only later that we all fell into the habit of referring to him as Don Cicatrice, and in a strange way the name suits him. He was badly hurt, and caring for him saved my sanity, for I know what it is like to lose a much-loved husband.'

Destine listened to all this in a rather stunned way. It seemed awful to think of this gracious woman torn heart and mind by such a terrible end to her husband. She looked so calm, so impeccable, so in control of her emotions – had she screamed, as Destine had? Had she cried out *murderer*?

'Was it an accident?' she asked quietly.

'We never really knew – it was presumed so. A fallen cigarette, perhaps, igniting the straw on the floor of the stables. But that is how my nephew came by his scar, for you are bound to be curious about him, and he is almost bound not to satisfy a fraction of your curiosity. There is a streak of irony in him, if not iron.'

Yet, thought Destine, he would have been acceptable as a husband for Cosima. Was it possible that he loved her? She tried to imagine him in love with a woman and could only visualise a man who might feel a strong desire but never any of the gentler emotions. Perhaps long ago they had been seared out of him at the time of the fire, and Cosima had known this and been swept off her feet by someone with charm and lies on his lips. Destine didn't think that Don Cicatrice would ever deceive with a lie; he would always be painfully frank about his feelings, as he had been last night, and this morning, when he had told her that he didn't want her here. It wasn't only that she was a threat to his aunt's peace of mind, it could be that she was a threat to his.

Destine's hands gripped each other . . . she was young, she was a woman, and there was no doubt at all in her mind that Don Cicatrice was very much a man, with that hard, definite virility that made Spaniards seem more masculine than other men. They had none of that thickening of face and body of European men in their thirties; their bodies remained sleek and lithe, and their features had an El Greco distinctness. The cruel glories and follies of Spain ran in their veins, and it showed.

'You seem,' said the Marquesa, with a faint touch of humour, 'to have taken a dislike to my nephew. He is an uncompromising man who wastes no words on idle flattery – in that he is the un-typical Latin, and it is accounted for by the fact that his paternal grandmother was from Australia, of all places. Her husband met her while travelling around the world; she was a remarkable woman who ran some kind of a hotel out in the wilds of that vast country. A tall, vivid-eyed woman, with a strong personality which she has passed on to Artez.'

'I see,' Destine was intrigued despite herself. 'So that accounts for his tallness. Spaniards have fine physiques but they aren't always so tall as your nephew – yet, despite that dash of Australian blood, he seems to dislike women of my type. He thinks we are dyed and decadent.'

The Marquesa broke into a smile. 'Long ago, before the women of Europe began to invade our beach resorts, the Latin had an idealised view of the fair Northerner. I'm afraid that ideal has fallen from its pedestal since the advent of the bikini, and the hunger for romance that many women of Europe bring to Spain. Have romance and modesty quite deserted your country and made our men take the view that European women are of easy virtue?'

Destine smiled ruefully. 'It's a phase that we are going through, I think. A reaction against the double standard that decrees that men may sow their wild oats but not women. I noticed in Madrid that lots of the girls were attired in European fashions and my godmother told me that the young men now date the girls without always asking permission of their parents. It would seem that modern ideas are spreading.'

'Ah yes, in Madrid.' The Marquesa spoke drily. 'But this is the south, Destine, and here the old ways still prevail. A young woman of the south still has to be careful of her reputation, otherwise she will not find a young man to marry her. The old courting ways still go on here at Xanas, and the parents still take a firm hand in the selection of a husband for a daughter, especially if she is pretty and has a fair dowry. You may find us very old-fashioned in this part of the world, if you are a very emancipated young woman. Are you?'

Destine shook her head. 'Too much liberation does make women seem graceless, and it makes the men bad-mannered. I quite appreciate Latin courtesy and always find the Conde de Calva beautifully mannered and always so impeccably turned out in those well-tailored suits of his, and those hand-made Spanish shoes. I think most Spaniards retain that grandee air which is so fascinating to Europeans. I think even the liberated females prefer gentlemen to boors, and that is probably why they flock to Spanish beaches. Even Spanish waiters are superbly mannered.'

'An inherited trait,' said the Marquesa, looking thoughtful. 'Just as our cruelty is inherited. We can be cruel, you know, Destine. Cosima's husband was cruel to her, and my own son – ' She broke off with a sigh. 'Anyway, I think we now understand each other a little better. I want you to be a friend to my daughter – if you can.'

'I shall certainly try, Señora Marquesa.'

'I warn you that it will not be easy, Destine. Her illness and the unhappiness over that man whom she married have left their mark on the personality of Cosima. Once she was a girl that anyone could like, but now she is hard to get close to. One has to be firm with her, otherwise she relapses into bouts of melancholia that are frightening. My nephew deals firmly with her – '

54

'I can imagine,' Destine couldn't resist saying.

'Don't mistake me.' The Marquesa looked severe for a moment. 'He doesn't resort to bullying, for he is fond of her. But he has a certain way with her and Cosima listens to him.'

'He is against the idea of an English nurse –' Destine bit her lip; he was against her for more reasons than one, but for all that some primitive response had been triggered off between them. Their mutual antipathy had set a spark to a dynamic sort of awareness; he didn't like her fair, Northern, modern look, no more than she liked his arrogance of height and personality, but he had kissed her and she was still shockingly aware of it. His face could never frighten her, but his touch had the power to terrify her. He disturbed her as no one had for a long time ... he touched her and what had been numb in her was suddenly tingling with life and pain.

'I hope he won't interfere –' Her voice sharpened. 'As your daughter's nurse, I hope I shan't be under his jurisdiction in any way? I – I don't think I could stand for that, Señora Marquesa.'

'Of course not,' she was reassured. 'My nephew is busy about the estate for most of the day, but he does like an hour with Cosima in the evenings. I think if you are successful with Cosima, he will be more than grateful. Since her accident they have become close, and I believe if she could forget that husband of hers and agree to a divorce – well, it would please me, and suit me, to see Cosima in the total care of Artez.'

'But isn't divorce awkward for Spanish people?' Destine asked. 'The Catholic laws are still very strict, aren't they?'

'The man she married is a Californian.' The Marquesa looked scornful. 'It could be arranged without too much trouble – he is there now, you know, and I have it on good authority that he is involved with another woman. I could pay for the evidence to get Cosima a divorce, but she refuses

55

to listen to the good sense of the argument. She remains besotted by the man, and we can but hope when she is feeling more herself that we can persuade her to cut free of him once and for all. I am no longer a young woman. I can't live for many more years, but my nephew is strong and in the prime of his manhood. It is, I confess to you, Destine, the dear wish of my heart that I should live to see those two safe together. He would be good to her ...'

'But isn't she paralysed, Señora Marquesa?' Destine spoke impulsively, unable to associate all that leashed power of the Don's with a woman who might always be condemned to a wheelchair. A vivid image of that lean and virile body flashed across her mind ... he was a man who would ride his horses like an Arab, and make love to a woman with passion in place of tenderness. Surely a woman like Cosima needed tenderness?

'There is always hope that she may one day regain partial use of her legs.' The Marquesa spoke hopefully, but her eyes remained bleak. 'What are you thinking, Destine, that men marry for physical reasons rather than those of the heart? *Quien sabe?* Many Spaniards take a mistress, and I see that you have noticed that my nephew is much of a man. That would not be important, for I should know that with the better part of him he would care for Cosima and be with her when he is needed. He would not be like that other one! In him the devil rules, but only now and then is the devil in charge of Artez. For the most part he is in charge of himself. He knows the taste of pain, and he and Cosima are linked by their Obregon blood, for his mother was my dear sister.'

The Marquesa gave a sigh and her slim hands looked frail as she linked them together, the heavy antique rings looking heavy on her fingers. 'In many ways this has been a family cursed by more sadness than happiness. The Obregon blood line is a very old one and it goes back a long way into the past, to a time of forebears who were not always–kind. It is whispered in Xanas that there is a curse on our family that will not be eradicated until the last male of the line is dead without a son to carry on the blood. In which case it might be for the good if Artez eventually becomes the husband of Cosima. They would be childless, so the curse, if there is one, would be ended. He is, you see, the last male of the line. The last man born into this family with Obregon blood in his veins. We live in a superstitious region, and there are people of the village who cross themselves when they see the scarred face of my nephew. They say that he carries the mark of the devil, and what use is it to tell them that he was burned in a fire as a young boy? They would only say that it was hellfire in which he burned.'

A faint smile stole back into the Marquesa's fine eyes. 'All of this must seem strange to you, Destine, coming from a world where everything is so up-to-date, and where all things are explained in specific terms by the psychologists. Here in Xanas the dark beliefs of the past have not yet been unveiled by the intellectuals and we have our *brujas* who practise their skills on the young and the old. They will provide a young girl with a love potion, or an old man with a remedy for his aches and pains, and the strange part is that very often these potions distilled from witchcraft are effective. I was even persuaded myself to let one of these old women see Cosima. I hoped, just a little. Artez, of course, was sceptical and the old woman went away in a huff, but you won't do that, will you, Destine? You will stay?'

'Yes, I'll stay.' Destine felt shocked by the desperation which had made this graceful and intelligent woman resort to the magic of a witch in order to try and cure Cosima. It was poliomyelitis which had attacked her nervous system, therefore she could never recover the full use of her lower body, which had been affected at the time of the attack. The invocation of spells would have no effect at all, and Destine bit back a smile as she visualised the scorn of Don

57

Cicatrice. Having hounded the old *bruja* out of the house it wouldn't worry him that she might cast one of her more vindictive spells over him. He might feel himself sufficiently damned, for there were people everywhere who turned quick eyes from a scar or a physical deformity.

'You will not depart in a huff if my nephew should ruffle your feathers?' The Marquesa smiled. 'I suspect that a few feathers have already flown, but he is like that. He courts no favour but speaks his mind, and it can be disconcerting to some people.'

'I'm sure it can,' said Destine, a trifle tartly, having already lost feathers in her struggle with him – not that she intended to describe that incident to his aunt. 'I think I can take his scoffs and his digs, but I wouldn't be happy if he interfered in any routine I set up for my patient. I'm a nurse, so I hope he won't treat me like a witch.'

'If you are good for Cosima, then he'll be as grateful as I shall.' The Marquesa rose to her feet. 'You have a nice voice, Destine, with a huskiness to it which is attractive. You also have a pleasing appearance. You will look more like a friend to Cosima than a nurse, for the last one was always bustling and rustling about in a starched uniform with an air of great importance. She exuded an air of the medicine cabinet and the temperature chart. I believe she unnerved Cosima, but you are different – I can but hope that one of our handsome young Spaniards does not whisk you from under our eyes.'

'There is no fear of that.' Destine spoke firmly as she rose to her feet. 'My work is my life, Señora Marquesa, and I shan't fall in love again. Love of that kind was killed for me when my husband died.'

'You say that, child, but destiny may have other ideas about your future. None of us, you know, can truly be sure of what even the next hour may bring. We hang suspended in a web of chance. We are creatures very much at the mercy of

58

the unknown. Our plans, our hopes, are toys that the gods play with.'

These words, spoken from the heart of a woman reared to Spanish fatalism, made Destine shiver a little. She felt suddenly very insecure, as if she felt herself actually suspended in mid-air like a moth on the globe of a lamp ... a vulnerable moth whose wings could be scorched, or pulled from her slim body. She had to believe that she was in control of her own future, but the Marquesa had shaken that belief. She looked about her, half afraid, and her eyes met those of the matadors in the Goya painting.

Dark, intent, with a gleam of the devil at their depths. Something seemed to prod her heart ... they were like the eyes of Don Cicatrice, and therefore like the eyes of Manolito.

'No,' she said huskily. 'I mean not to love again, and I have not been out with a man for two years. I shan't break that rule here at Xanas. Your handsome Spaniards won't be encouraged by the coldness of my emotions where men are concerned. Latin men like women who have hearts to take and break. My heart was buried with Matthew –'

'Matthew?' The Marquesa took her up. 'That was your husband's name?'

'Yes.' Destine's nerves seemed to jangle with alarm. Had she given herself away by letting out Matt's name?

'Is it an uncommon name in England?' The Marquesa was staring at Destine. 'Not often heard there?'

'Oh – not uncommon at all,' Destine said quickly. 'As it is a Biblical name, many people give it to their sons. It's a nice name, but certainly not rare in England.'

'Then your husband was named Matthew Chard?'

'Yes.' The lie slipped from Destine's lips involuntarily, for the real truth couldn't be told to this woman who had already suffered so much. 'May I now see the Señora Arandas? Is she expecting me?'

'Yes, she is probably all keyed up for the meeting. Her maid helps her to bathe, and she will have had some coffee and pecked at the good breakfast which Victoria provides. If only she would eat more! Do come this way, Destine. Her suite is on the ground floor, of course. They are connecting rooms devised from an indoor chapel, which we rarely use as I prefer to attend Mass at the church in the village. It provides an outing for me, and I fear that neither Cosima nor Artez are particularly devout. My daughter lost much of her faith when her illness cost her that man whom she still believes she loves, and my nephew is a man who believes only in what he can see and touch.'

They crossed the hall, which beneath the thick white archways was floored with arabesque tiles that provided deep rich colour in contrast to the walls. Here and there were ironwork screens, a tracery of patterns that were intricate until one looked closely and saw leopard heads and eagle claws and the running shape of a gazelle.

'Much of the *casa* is Moresque,' said the Marquesa. 'Those tiles and screens, and the way the cedarwood doors are fitted and carved. The Moors had great artistry, and they built these walls of thick solid stone in order to keep out the heat of the full southern sun, but you will notice that they softened the cloistered effect by adding the delicate tracery of iron and the oriental tiles. Would it surprise you, Destine, to learn that the Obregons trace their ancestry back to the days of the Moors? The family records include the name of Tarik, the one-eyed hawk, who was a kind of *conquistadore* for the Sultan of Morocco. Very colourful days, with courts here in the south that rivalled those in Baghdad and Babylon.'

Destine thought of the nephew of this house, the hawk-like pride of the profile, the deep arch to the brows, the flare to the nostrils, the glint to his teeth against the sun-bitten skin that made his jagged scar stand out bone-white. He had all the lean ferocity of an Arab; totally dedicated to his family, and ruthless towards those whom he considered outsiders.

She was such, and more so. She had reason to hate the Obregons, and he would watch her every move as a hawk might watch a hare.

'No, what you tell me doesn't surprise me in the least,' she said. 'That hint of the Moorish hawk is in your nephew, in his look and in his ways, I think.'

'A throwback, eh?' His aunt smiled as she paused in front of carved double doors. 'I don't think you miss much, Destine.'

'It's part of my profession, Señora Marquesa. We are taught to be observant.'

'Good. I like a young woman who has her wits about her, but who, at the same time, is not a busybody. And now meet my daughter!'

The Marquesa swung open the carved doors and they entered what had once been the main chancel of the chapel. Destine caught her breath at the subdued beauty of the place, the *mudejar* ceiling of interlacing pieces of cedarwood, richly painted and carved. The oriel windows through which the sun slanted in a myriad colours on to the floor tiled in black and white. There was a sense of coolness and peace, to which homely touches had been added by placing long seats under the windows cushioned in ruby velvet, and there were bookcases and Murillo paintings of waifs and angels upon the walls.

'It's very lovely,' Destine breathed. 'So very different from working in a hospital.'

'Yes, when the renovations were done, we left the general impression of a chancel and added the comforts of a livingroom. Cosima rarely leaves her apartment, and as you can see there is an archway that leads out to her own private patio. She will be there now. Her maid Anaya would have settled her there. Come, let us go out to her. I am sure she has heard

61

our voices, and is wondering about her new English nurse.'

Yes, thought Destine. It was rather like a room of secrets with a whispering gallery, and again she felt a sense of the past as they stepped out from the archway on to the patio, where old stone walls were hung with bright shawls of flowers; a place of nooks and niches and scented myrtle. Of silvery olive leaves rustling like tiny castanets, and a brilliant fuchsia with its tiny fire dancers.

There beneath the shade of Monk's Pepper rested Señora Arandas on a long cane chair, her legs covered by a shawl of Iberian lacework. She gazed straight at Destine with large, incredibly dark eyes that made the golden pallor of her skin all the more transparent, and her features all the more fragile and defined. She wore pale chiffon for coolness, and her silky dark hair was drawn back from her face. She might once have been very pretty, but now her eyes and her features lacked life and any real interest in other people.

'You are my new nurse?' she said, and she spoke in English, in an accent that would have been attractive had there been any life in her voice. 'I suppose Madre has been telling you all about my *triste* disposition, and warning you that I weep at the drop of a lace handkerchief? Are you going to be severe with me, like the last *ama*? I will call you *ama* or *tata* as the mood takes me. The other one she didn't like this at all and wished me to be always correct. Are you a correct person, Nurse Inglesa?'

'I don't think so, *señora*.' Destine smiled, and looking at this Latin girl she knew why Don Cicatrice might be in love with her. She was the total opposite to all that he was; fragile, dependent on others for her content, and almost as lacking in vitality as a pale and lovely doll. He was so abundantly vital that he would feel a strong sense of protectiveness towards Cosima. Every facet of life would have some meaning for him, but this girl no longer cared whether she lived or died.

62

It was a sad situation and Destine was surprised that she was moved by it, for this was Manolito's sister, and she should be feeling nothing at all for any of these people. She was, however, conscious of a wish to take the girl's thin hands in her own, imparting sympathy rather than antipathy.

'I don't mind what you call me, *señora*,' she said, 'so long as we get along and can establish a good working relationship. I want very much to help you get well.'

'Why should you want that?' Cosima looked sceptical. 'You are a stranger to me and can have no feeling for what I feel. You will be well paid for what you do and that is all that really matters to you. In fact, you won't stay very long— none of them do. They find Xanas too far from amusements —and they soon learn that Don Cicatrice is not to be flirted with. One nurse, poor fool, was actually afraid of him!'

'I can assure you that I'm not afraid of your cousin.' Destine said it with assurance, but only in her own heart could she know that a strange fear of the man did lurk in her veins. It wasn't a physical fear, for it had nothing to do with his face that had been so cruelly marred while he was still only a boy. But it was there, and it made her set her chin more firmly and look her patient proudly in the eyes. 'As I told your mother, *señora*, I am only concerned to do my duty to the best of my ability, and I do assure you that I'm quite a good nurse, and though I shan't bustle around you with medicine bottles and charts, I shall expect you to abide by what I feel is good for you, and what I feel is bad.'

'My dear Madre,' Cosima glanced at her mother with a faint arousal of humour in her eyes under-circled by shadows that revealed that she slept with the aid of drugs. 'I do believe that we have another martinet on our hands. Oh, what a bore! And just as I was hoping to be left alone—after all, Don Cicatrice did assure me that English women were more bent on pleasure than anything else. Aren't you here, Nurse, like all the others were, to flirt with our handsome men?'

'My flirting days are over, and we must understand each other, *señora*. If I am to be your nurse, then you must accept that my orders take precedence over your cousin's. I am sure that he has your welfare close to his heart, but he isn't a doctor, nor is he an absolute authority on the many women of my country who work fearfully hard and aren't forever chasing after handsome Latins. It isn't fair to judge me in advance, is it?'

Cosima looked unmoved by this and gave a delicate yawn. 'I feel as if I have slept with a weight on my face.'

'Aren't you feeling very well this morning, *carina*.' The Marquesa bent over her daughter and gently cradled her colourless face. 'Those great shadows beneath your eyes do worry me—once upon a time you had such sparkling eyes, and now they are so listless.'

'How many pills do you take in order to sleep, *señora*?' Destine walked round to the other side of the cane lounger and took hold of her patient's wrist. The pulse was nervously erratic, and that too was an indication of too much intake of a sleeping drug.

Cosima stared up at her as she counted the pulsebeats.

'Well, *señora*,' she said again, 'Is it two pills, or three?'

'It's as many as will bring sleep,' Cosima rejoined. 'Deep, dark sleep, where I forget everything—like going down under the sea. No dreams, Nurse. No yesterday and no tomorrow.'

When Cosima said this, in almost a yearning voice, her mother glanced at Destine with a touch of desperation. Neither of them could mistake what lay in Cosima's words . . . the longing to drop forever into sleep so that she need never awake to face what each day held, the fact that she was an invalid who could no longer ride horses, dance, or be held in the arms of the man who had deserted her.

A fierce clutch of pity caught at Destine's heart, but she kept her expression composed, as she had been taught. The very last thing that she must reveal was the sympathy of someone who had felt a similar despair; who had wanted not to wake in the mornings to face life bereft of what had made it pleasing and secure.

First and foremost Destine had to be a nurse when Cosima spoke in this fashion, and taking a look at the breakfast tray that was mostly untouched on the nearby cane table, she said briskly: 'It seems such a pity not to eat that delicious-looking orange. Look how beautifully it has been peeled for you, and cut like a water-lily. It looks exactly like a flower – why don't you imagine that you're eating one, plucking the petals one by one?'

'Why don't you, if the orange looks so inviting?' Cosima said rudely. 'I don't happen to be hungry – it's lack of exercise, so I am told by our good doctor. I am given vitamins in place of the food I just can't face in the morning. I keep telling Madre that good food is being wasted, but still they bring the tray. What is it done for? Just to pretend that I am still alive instead of half dead?'

'Cosima, please don't speak like that.' The Marquesa looked very distressed. 'We do all we can for you, for you are very much alive to us and we love you.'

'Am I alive to Miguel? Does he love me?' A twisted smile made it uncertain whether Cosima would cry or scream. 'I wish all of you would let me fade away naturally like a withered flower – you are driving me to do what I know would damn my soul in your eyes, Madre. One night I shall swallow all the pills.'

'And then have to go through the torture of having your stomach pumped out, *señora*?' Destine asked. 'I have watched this operation, and it's far from pleasant and is, in fact, an ugly procedure. It hurts and it lacks dignity. Is that what you would like to endure, for if you took the pills you don't imagine that I'd let you slip away, do you?'

Cosima stared again at Destine, as if trying to see the real person under the façade of neat hair and dress, and a face drilled into a mask of cool composure. 'I am told that your husband died young,' she said. 'Is this so?'

'Yes, *señora*. My husband died on our wedding day.'

'And didn't you want to die? Or did it compensate that you still had the full use of your body and could find someone else to love you?'

'I knew great grief,' Destine said quietly. 'And I also knew that nothing could compensate me for the loss of M – my husband. He promised to be a brilliant doctor, and he was enormously kind. I don't expect to find his like again, *señora*.'

'But you had your health – your work,' said Cosima relentlessly. 'What do you think I have? I was never trained in anything but charm and how to manage horses and young men. Now I am about as charming as a stick of wood, with legs to match, and a heart to go with them. I lie about on this patio, watching the birds as they fly and mate, and counting the hours until I can drop again into bottomless sleep. It is truly a life to envy, is it not?'

'I have seen polio victims so stricken, *señora*, that they must spend their days and nights in an iron lung. Some can move but a finger, and one such man has written a book, typing it himself with that single finger.'

'Perhaps he has a brain to start off with,' Cosima rejoined. 'All I had to give was myself, and the man to whom I gave myself wanted an entire woman, not one with half her body a dead weight. I shall never blame Miguel for leaving me. I understand why he left. He was too full of life to be able to endure only half a wife. Why should he make a saint of himself? If he had stayed he would only have gone behind my back for his pleasures. As it was he departed openly without deceit. It was brave of him to do that.'

'It was selfish.' Destine couldn't hold back the words. 'Real people don't run out on their obligations, *señora*. They

66

face up to them, not being saintly but being true to themselves and to the person who has been hurt through no fault
of her own.'

'You speak like a romantic.' Cosima looked cynical. 'I
thought English people were realists—their newspapers and
magazines are always boasting that this is so.'

'Newspapers and magazines, *señora*, are in the hands of
editors who are probably afraid to admit that romance is
not quite as dead as the dodo. They would like to kill it,
for it's easier to write about sordid things.'

'Yet you, as a nurse, must have seen many shocking
things.' Cosima gave Destine a curious glance. 'You don't
look the typical nurse of my experience, and that has not
been inconsiderable in the last three years. Do you really
think you are going to find me endurable, and Xanas, which
is so deep in the south that you will still hear Moorish
music, and the tinkle of tiny bells on the ankle chain of
Zahra, the slave girl who haunts our fountain court. We are
a strange family, Nurse. We live much in the past, and you
are from London, which is one of the most cosmopolitan
capitals of the world. I predict that you will run away from
us in a matter of days.'

Destine didn't argue with Cosima. This was Manolito's
family and she still wasn't certain why she had decided to
stay. She only knew that she felt challenged by the Don, and
by this Spanish girl who had once been vivacious and active,
and who now only wished to find a dreamless oblivion.

'I'm not afraid of the country, and I'm intrigued by your
ghost,' she said. And then she tensed as Cosima suddenly
switched her glance to beyond Destine's shoulder; she felt
compelled to glance in that direction, and there by a palm
tree whose base was swathed in bougainvillaea was no
ghost but the very vital figure of Don Cicatrice. The smoke
of a cheroot drifted about his dark features, and his eyes
seemed to be mocking her.

'So our nurse is unafraid of ghosts,' he drawled. 'Perhaps it's down-to-earth people who make her tremble, eh?'

'Am I supposed to be a trembling leaf in your presence, señor?' she asked, while fury swept through her as she looked at him and knew that he was sharing the memory of their last encounter. They both knew that she had felt weak with fear of him, and she longed once more to strike that derisive smile from his lips. She felt that he would do everything to make her stay here an impossible one, and a blue flame lit her eyes . . . a fighting flame that made his eyes go narrow, so that the black lashes met and made him sinister.

'We'll see,' he said, 'just how much you can stand of us.'

'Artez, for heaven's sake don't lose us another nurse,' the Marquesa exclaimed. 'I really begin to think that you have some ingrained prejudice against nurses—perhaps it goes back to your boyhood. As I explained to Destine, you were very much hurt at that time and—'

'Destine?' he broke in, and his gaze arrogantly mocked her. 'So that is your name? I wondered what the D stood for. D is such a significant letter, is it not? Standing for dearest and darling; devil and death.'

'Artez, go about your business,' his aunt said sharply. 'You will drive Destine away before she has had a chance to get to know us. We really aren't as bad as he would paint us, child. He is just the typical Spaniard who believes that a family should try and heal its own and not call upon strangers.'

'How fearfully insular and old-fashioned of him,' Destine said tartly. 'It's the Moorish influence, I suppose? The high walls and the maze of courts that confuse the stranger who dares to trespass. Perhaps the señor is afraid that I shall be more successful than he has been at encouraging Señora Arandas to look forward to the future?'

'Is that your specialty, Nurse?' he drawled, and he looked

directly into her eyes, reminding her with that look that she had claimed to care only about the past; that her love lay locked in its embrace, and made of her a woman who could never forgive and forget.

'I am a nurse.' She flung up her chin as she looked at him. 'I never forget that my first duty is my patient's welfare. If you're afraid that I shall harm the *señora* in any way, then you needn't be.'

'Of course not, Artez.' The Marquesa went to him and took his arm. 'Destine comes to us with the best of qualifications, so we may safely leave Cosima in her hands.'

'Let us hope so,' he said, walking with his aunt from the patio.

Destine watched him go with an acute sense of relief. No one in her life before had ever made her feel that her mind could be looked into, and her heart laid open for hard fingers to probe.

'You don't like him, do you?' Cosima gave her weary laugh. 'Is it his face that makes you look as if you had just encountered Satan himself?'

'I'm not that foolish.' Destine gave a faint shiver. 'Your cousin doesn't like me, *señora*.'

'Does that scratch your vanity, Nurse?'

'I'm not vain, I hope.'

'How unusual in a girl with such shining hair and a skin so touchable. Most men must find you very appealing, with such hair and that slender figure. Has it come as a shock that Don Cicatrice is the exception?'

'It doesn't surprise me in the least that he dislikes me. The antipathy is mutual, as it sometimes is for no accountable reason. I don't think your cousin is much in sympathy with the human race.'

'A cynic, eh?'

'Very much so.' Destine watched as a white kitten with a black tail leapt on to Cosima's lap and began to purr as it

69

snuggled into her thin arms. 'That's a very pretty cat, *señora*.'

'My cousin gave him to me, for company when he is not about. I call him Domino, and it will be part of your duty to see that those girls from the kitchen don't forget his saucer of milk and his sliced kidneys. These girls think only about – ah, but I am just being envious of their youth and their ability to laugh and dance at the *feria*. Life is strange, is it not, Destine?'

'Very strange, *señora*, in some ways.'

'Would it strike you as strange that Don Cicatrice loves me?'

'No.' Destine shook her head. 'We all need to love someone.'

'Yet you say that love is over for you; done with.'

'It is,' said Destine. 'My husband was a good man.'

'So you like only good men?' Cosima smiled, almost to herself. 'You make me feel so much older than you, and yet we are of an age. Dear Nurse, you have yet to learn that until a woman has loved a devil she hasn't really lived.'

CHAPTER FOUR

SOMEHOW a week had passed, and for most of that time Destine had been with her patient, who had developed a cold and therefore needed the extra attention essential for someone who couldn't take physical exercise, one of the best ways of preventing a cold from going to the chest.

Because of feeling so run down Cosima was peevish and inclined to pick little quarrels with everyone, her nurse in particular. But Destine was too accustomed to the moods of sick people to take very much notice, and in the end Cosima sulkily smiled at her and told her she was of the stuff that martyrs were made.

'I thought you would find this house like a prison and wouldn't stay here,' she said, dabbing at her nose with a lace-edged handkerchief. 'I wonder what changed your mind? It couldn't be that you found my cousin handsome unless you are the type that likes a manly form and isn't concerned with charming good looks.'

'As I have told you before, *señora*, I am not concerned with men at all.' Destine tidied a mound of magazines and replaced the lid on a box of fondants. 'Would I have come all this way to work if I couldn't live without male company?'

Cosima shrugged her shoulders, clad in a robe of chiffon silk edged at the full sleeves with soft beige fur. 'Were I in your shoes and able to walk, I would walk out of here and go where the life and the gaiety are. It's hell on earth to be tied to an invalid chair, only half a woman instead of a whole one. Who could desire me? When I look at you, Destine, I am filled with envy, and I wonder why you endure someone like me when you are free to do as you wish. Were you so in love with your husband that you have no desire for love any more? What an unnatural state of mind and body when you are really a most attractive person—why, you are like a nun who has taken the vow of chastity, and you must intrigue Don Cicatrice for all that he looks at you with eyes of irony.'

'I'm quite sure his feelings are centred on you, *señora.*' More than once had Cosima probed in this way, as if jealous of her cousin's love for her even if she didn't return it. She had to be sure that he wasn't interested in anyone else, and Destine was only too ready to reassure her that nothing but a mutual antipathy existed between herself and the tall, scarred Spaniard.

'Your cousin doesn't strike me as a Don Juan,' she said, pausing at the dressing-table to admire the toiletries of white jade and amethyst-blue. 'I should think that once he has set his heart on a woman he would want her and no one else.'

'I wonder why you are so sure,' Cosima drawled. 'Does he confide in you?'

'Heavens, no!' Destine swung round from the dressing-table and her eyes were brilliantly startled. 'We hardly meet, let alone speak. He disapproves of me, and equates me with the sun-loungers of the Costa Brava.'

'Even though you have spent a week in my sickroom?' Cosima gave a laugh that broke off into a sigh. 'It is said that women are the mystery of life, but let me tell you, Destine, that here in Spain it is the men. In this particular region they are half Arab and the strange ways of the desert haunt their blood. I warn you that Don Cicatrice is not like the young doctors of your English hospitals, and even though I have known him all my life, I don't profess to know him. Sometimes he—he actually frightens me—'

'You?' Destine exclaimed. 'But he cares for you, *señora.*'

'I don't mean that he would harm me—no, that is too

72

ridiculous a thought. But he is so deep, and that is why I have always been a little afraid of him. He would, I think, break a woman's neck if she took his love and then played with it. The love that he feels for me is not of that sort, it is more of an affection, a compassion – ah yes, Destine, he can be compassionate, for he's a Spaniard. The veins of cruelty and compassion run side by side in the men of my country, whom you probably equate with the matador. Is this not so? For me this cousin of mine typifies *mal angel*, and I am thankful that he gives me the sweet side of his heart rather than the reverse. I could never be woman enough to pacify all that is in the heart of Don Cicatrice. I could never be angel and devil in one body, and that is what he needs.'

Destine didn't argue with Cosima, for there was too much truth in what she said. He was the kind of man who might be gentle with a woman hurt, or a child crying, but when it came to passion he would be the absolute master of the woman in his arms and he would bring out the devil in her.

Destine had decided from the start that he was a man to be avoided, but once Cosima was over her cold and feeling quite well again, she no longer wished to dine alone with her nurse and Destine had to brace herself for more social contact with the man.

The family dined at eight-thirty in the evening and she was ordered to join them.

Anaya, the maid who had been with Cosima since she was a girl, was in charge of her mistress's toilette, so Destine was able to get ready for dinner without rushing under the shower and into a dress.

Her trunk had arrived from Madrid a few days ago, so she was able to select a dress from the half dozen formals she had brought with her. Her choice was a long-sleeved lace blouse which she had purchased in Madrid, where the lace was handmade, and she matched it to a long velvet skirt in aubergine.

73

After she had arranged her hair into a calot and lightly coloured her lips, she was pleased to see that she could hold her own with the Obregons. She looked quite chic, in fact and her hair had a glistening quality. It still rankled that the Don had taken her for a bottle blonde . . . what a fearful cynic he was, and such people were so armoured that it was almost impossible to scratch them in return.

A glance at her wristwatch showed her that it was almost eight o'clock, when the family assembled in the *salita* off the dining-room for their aperitif. Though this was a family that lived in the heart of the south, its habits were civilized, even though Destine had reason to know that under the skin they weren't quite so suave and had a streak of ruthlessness in them.

Holding her long skirt above her ankles, Destine made her way down the long curve of the staircase, with a balustrade of iron wrought into arabesqued patterns. The Moorish lamps were alight along the vista of archways, and as she paused on the stairs and gazed downwards it was as if she had left the modern world and wandered into another era.

She saw a strange beauty in the coloured lamps, in the spiky flames of the flowers growing in great pots against the white walls, in the lovely tiles framed in lacy ironwork. She feasted her eyes on the interlacing arches, their columns fluted and inset with Moorish script . . . it did seem feasible that a slave girl might wander these halls, the tiny bells making a soft seductive music on her ankles . . . and at that moment, sending a shiver all the way through her body, a shadow shifted out from an archway into a pool of golden light and Destine saw a white-clad arm lifted lazily to carry a thin cigar to lips set in a dark, masculine face.

He didn't say a word, he just stood there and looked at her, his eyes as inscrutable as the shadows which had concealed him from her. He wore a crisp white dinner-jacket over narrow black trousers, and he wore them with super-

74

lative ease. There was a gleam of bloodstone at his cuffs, and yet again Destine had an impression of sophistication that could be as easily slipped off as the tailored jacket that he wore.

'Good evening, *señor.*' Destine collected her composure like a cloak around her and descended the last few stairs with an assumption of ease. She would never get used to his almost sinister distinction, and his way of coming and going as silently as a jungle jaguar tracking its prey.

'You look startled,' he said. 'Did you expect to see the ghost of the *casa?* I thought you said you were unafraid of them?'

'You seem to think, *señor,* that everything I say should be queried and questioned by you. Are there inquisitors in your ancestry as well as Moors who kept slave girls?'

His white teeth clenched the cigar, and smoke writhed and curled over his lean features as he allowed a silence to hold the two of them in a kind of suspense. The scent of tropical foliage drifted in from the gardens and mingled with the rich smoke, and Destine felt again that stirring of fear and fascination. He knew of her tragic involvement with Manolito and that made a secret between them, and secrets were intimate things.

'I am the last man in Spain to deny that our history has been a cruel one,' he said. 'But it amuses me that your own people should consider themselves angels just because of a fair skin and hair. Standing there you look divinely good and graceful, but we both know, don't we, that you know how to hate and you hate me and see in me all the sins of Manolito.'

'That I feel antipathetic—that we both feel it, for each other, should set your mind at rest, *señor.* In such circumstances I shan't be tempted to run after you for your protection and riches.'

He quirked a brow into even more of a devilish arc, and smoke curled from the lips that smiled briefly and cynically.

75

'I have never felt less protective towards any woman, *señora*, and not merely because you hate me. The hatred of a woman is a gnat bite, as we say in Spain. Hating and loving are too closely related for anyone to really know the difference.'

'What nonsense!' Destine spoke sharply. 'I could never mistake one for the other – I felt hatred stab sheer through me when your cousin stepped alive out of his car while my husband lay there, mangled, blind with blood, dead! I could have killed him myself! I – I wished him dead!'

'And it came to pass.' The words came with a sinister softness from the lips of Don Cicatrice, drifting through space with the smoke from his *cigarro*.

'It was on the cards for someone who lived as he did.' Destine flung back her head and the golden lamplight shimmered on her hair and cast gold shadows over her white skin. Her eyes had the density of midnight in that moment, and there was a sudden ripping sound as her fingers tore in two the lace handkerchief that she was holding. 'He gambled with lives and he paid the price. He was bad and he killed someone good and kind – someone capable of saving lives. Matthew was a surgeon, did you know that? Your cousin was a Latin playboy – oh, to hell with him! I hope he's in purgatory!'

'My dear young woman, hell and heaven are here on earth.'

Destine stared at Don Cicatrice, the torn handkerchief gripped in her fingers. 'You're a Spaniard, so how can you believe that?' she said.

'I'm a cynic.' He shrugged his shoulders. 'And I had an English mother.'

'But the Marquesa told me that she and your mother were sisters.'

'Stepsisters,' he corrected. 'Their father was twice married, and his English daughter was my mother. An excellent match was arranged for her, but she found that she loved neither

76

my father nor me, and not long after I was born she left both of us. I came into the care of the Marquesa because my father was always a busy man. He was an administrator of public works, who was later stood up against a wall by the communists and shot dead for being loyal to his king.'

A silence prevailed, and then the Don moved fully into the lamplight and his scar stood out in jagged detail against his swarthy skin. 'Yes, *señora*, Spain is a land of saints and sinners, and it is known to have a most curious effect upon foreign women who come here. You had best beware, had you not?'

'Yes,' she said, in a voice not fully aware of what he implied, for she was still held by the personal things he had just told her. 'What became of your mother, *señor*? Do you ever see her?'

'She married an Englishman and lives in a place called the Chiltern Hills, and now I never see her.'

'Why – ?' Destine broke off her question, for one look at his adamant face was enough to tell her that he had too much pride to seek recognition or love of a woman who had abandoned him all those years ago. She understood, and yet it seemed so sad, somehow, to allow old hurts to go on giving pain.

Then Destine caught her breath, for she was like him in that respect – she couldn't forgive, or forget. Hating what had hurt you could somehow be a shield against further pain, and she dropped her glance from his face and walked with him in the direction of the *salita*.

The doors into this room were impressively carved and standing open to frame the interior, with chandeliers as chiselled as jewels in their beauty, hung from a *mudejar* ceiling of interlaced sections of cedarwood, varying in colour from near black to honey-gold. The ruby damask of the carved sofas glowed against the panelled walls, and lovely green Mallorca decanters shone on an antique side-table.

77

Across the floor lay carpets in dusky oriental colours, and altogether the effect was one of great charm, softening for Destine the mood she had drifted into, alone with the Don in the shadows of the hall ... alone with a man whose scars were more than skin deep.

She caught her breath, for this was the first time she had entered the *salita*. 'How charming!' She couldn't help saying it, and the Marquesa caught her words and turned from the man to whom she was talking and smiled at Destine.

'Ah, this is our Señora Chard who is nurse and *compañera* to Cosima. Come and be introduced to a friend of ours who comes to Spain to buy seed bulls for his farm in Wales.'

Destine approached at the invitation and found herself facing a muscular man who was almost as dark-haired as the Don. His name was Lugh Davidson and he looked at her with a gleam of surprise in his dark grey eyes. Swiftly he looked her up and down, and smile lines appeared beside his eyes.

'Why did I not have a nurse like you when I had my appendix out?' he asked. 'I am most pleased to meet you, Miss Chard.'

'It's Mrs. Chard,' she said at once. 'And do the Spanish really allow their famous bulls to go out of the country? I thought they were mostly used in the arenas for stickpins.'

His lips twitched, and he cast a quizzical look at the tall figure who appeared with a glass of sherry for Destine. 'Did you catch that one, *amigo*?' he asked. 'I would say that this young lady is an opponent of the *corrida* rather than a supporter, unlike some of those other female visitors to Spain who sit in the best seats yelling for the poor brute's ears.'

The Don's dark eyes flicked Destine's face as she accepted from him the flute of tawny sherry. 'Nurse Chard is quite convinced,' he said, in his most sardonic tone of voice, 'that the men of Spain are still like they were in the days of the *conquistadores*. Ruthless, you know, and rather sinister.'

With these words he moved away again, to play courtier to Cosima on one of the ruby-brocaded sofas, delicately distracting in honey-brown silk, her only adornment a heavy gold Spanish cross on a gold chain.

'A pity about that lovely creature,' said Lugh Davidson. 'Will she ever walk again, Nurse Chard?'

Destine shook her head. 'The greatest pity is that her husband didn't stand by her. Loyalty and love are the best medicine in the world and she could have been made to feel – well, a woman. As it is she feels that she is no more use to a man and she broods about it.'

'Artez is fond of her.' Lugh twirled his sherry glass in his hard-looking fingers. 'He's a strange fellow in some respects, but he might have made her a good husband. At least he wouldn't have left her when she lost the use of her legs. Life takes odd twists and turns, don't you think?'

'Indeed it does, Mr. Davidson.' Destine cast a brief look at the Don, who was leaning down protectively to catch what his cousin was saying to him, and there flashed through her mind remembrance of what he had said about feeling nothing protective with regard to her. She could stand up for herself, and any encounter between them would be *pidiendo guerra* – asking for war!

It surprised Destine that there were several other guests for dinner, for she hadn't thought that the Obregons were all that sociable. The high white walls of the *casa*, and the wrought-iron grilles at its windows, seemed to shut people out and made it seem that the family kept much to themselves.

She learned, however, that Lugh Davidson was staying in the neighbourhood with these Spanish people, who were the owners of the *finca* which had for sale the pair of seed bulls in which he was interested. Destine could only surmise that such bulls were enormously expensive, which gave her a clue as to the wealth of the Welshman. Her companion at the dinner table, he talked about his big stone farm in the hills

79

of Brecon, and because he was not a flirtatious man Destine enjoyed his company, and had no idea that they seemed to be isolated in a pool of candlelight from the tall, gold-wrought candelabrum on the table.

Beside his darkness she looked inordinately fair, and her eyes were very blue and intent as he described the beauty of those Welsh hills.

'You must find southern Spain a great contrast,' she said, smiling as she ate the delicious dessert of sliced tropical fruits with cream.

'It's the climate which is the greatest contrast,' he said. 'Don't you find the sun rather overpowering yourself, being so fair-skinned?'

'I've not yet been out in the full sun –' Suddenly Destine glanced across the table at Cosima, the massive carving of the chair in which she sat making her seem extra fragile. In that moment it struck Destine that she had promised to stay only a week at the *casa*, and that week was now over and she had to decide about tomorrow. She could leave, or she could stay, and either decision could bring regret with it.

She knew that forcibly as she sat there at the Marquesa's table, and her hand shook slightly as she lifted her wineglass and put her lips to the rim.

Inadvertently, and yet perhaps driven to it by the trend of her thoughts, her eyes slid to the figure seated beside her patient ... her nerves jolted, for his eyes locked with hers across the candlelit table, above the tawny gilt of the wine in the glass she was holding. She almost dropped it, and that would have been awful, the wine spilling over the lace cloth and staining it.

'Don't look at me like that!' she wanted to cry out. 'If you're reading my thoughts ... you know that it's you ... you who makes my decision such a hard one!'

His brow arched and his eyes mocked what he had seen, that she had almost spilled her wine because their eyes interlocked and a dramatic fusion of thought had set them apart for a few wild seconds from everyone else at the table.

She glanced away from him and she knew, now, that if she left Xanas it would be an act of flight from Don Cicatrice. He would know it, too, that she was running away from the disturbing effect that he had on her, and it would seem like a victory for him that he had made her run away.

Her chin tilted. To the devil with him! Cosima needed someone who could deal with her moods of depression, for if they weren't dealt with, then the Marquesa would have more heartache to hide behind a graciously brave smile.

At the conclusion of the long Spanish meal, Destine quietly approached Cosima and murmured that it really was time that she went to bed. 'You'll feel so wrung out in the morning if you overdo things, *señora*.'

'Yes,' said a decisive voice above Destine's head. 'Your nurse is right, *cara*. Time for bed!' Long arms reached down and gathered Cosima easily into their embrace. There in his strong arms Cosima smiled good-night at the guests of her mother, and without protest she allowed him to carry her to the chapel rooms that were now her ground-floor apartment.

Destine followed them and noticed that Cosima's weight had no more effect on the Don than if she had been an infant. He strode effortlessly beneath the archways of the hall in the direction of Cosima's rooms, pausing so that Destine might open the doors. Then he carried his cousin through the sitting-room archway into the luxurious bedroom, where he placed her on the bed so that she fell back with a slight smile against the pillows.

'How strong you are, *mio*,' she said, gazing up at him with the lamplight on her dark shining hair. Each night that lovely head of hair was brushed fifty times by Anaya, and as Destine stood quietly by she saw the eyes of Don Cicatrice steal over his cousin's raven hair.

81

'I only seem so in comparison to you, *cara*,' he rejoined. 'You must strive to get really well – tonight you had a nice time, eh? It was good to see our friends, was it not?'

'Not forgetting Señor Davidson.' Cosima glanced lazily at Destine. 'My dear, you appeared to like his company and his conversation. We all noticed how absorbed you were in each other, did we not, cousin?'

'It was a nice surprise to meet someone from my side of the ocean.' Destine strove not to look at the Don, for her thoughts about him had put her nerves on edge and she wanted him to be gone from the room, taking his disturbing aura with him. He was too mocking, shrewd, and faintly cruel for her to be able to cope with him tonight.

'You must get your rest, *señora*,' she said. 'It is very late.'

Cosima glanced at the little Limoges clock on her bedside table, and pulled a faintly sulky mouth. 'Oh, what a bore it is to be in the hands of a nurse, especially when there used to be a time when I could dance till three in the morning. Now I can't walk to my own bed and have to be carried to it, like a baby.'

'Stop the fussing and have a good night.' Don Cicatrice took his cousin's hands into his own and bending his tall head he kissed each hand on the back of the wrist. 'Behave and I may take you for a drive to the Castros *finca* this coming Sunday. You would like that?'

'Indeed I would, *mio*.' Cosima's fingers clung eagerly to his. 'Make it a promise and don't suddenly find some task in the fields or the office that must be done. You have your foreman Pascual and have no real need to be always so busy. Promise!'

'If it will make you happy.' A smile flickered on his lips. 'Tonight you looked very lovely, *cara*.'

At this compliment a flush of pleasure came into Cosima's cheeks. 'You are gallant to say so, cousin. It's been a long time since a man noticed that I am not quite hideous.'

'Little foolish one.' He brushed a hand across her hair. 'You were always a lovely Latin girl, and now you must obey orders and get your beauty sleep—'

'Artez—!'

He quirked an eyebrow. 'It isn't often that you call me that, Cosima. I begin to forget the name, I am referred to so often as the scarred one.'

'Artez,' she softened her voice, 'may Destine come with us on Sunday? It would be nice for her to see Señor Davidson once again, and I am sure she would enjoy the drive after being cooped up in my rooms for the past week. She isn't so bad, you know, for a nurse.'

He swung a look at Destine, so swiftly that she was unable to avoid his eyes and the way they had of stabbing into her thoughts. Instantly she had rejected the idea of intruding upon him and Cosima and was about to make an excuse when he smoothly disposed of it.

'Yes, Cosima should have her nurse in attendance. You will like the *finca, señora,* and the sleek bulls that go to the breeding farms instead of the arenas. As it happens we are not all keen on the butchery of fine animals, or the soulless slaughter of aged horses, and you must blame the tourist trade for some of the bloodier sides of the sport. The blood on the sand seems to send some of them into ecstasies, especially the women, who have doubtless never experienced any ecstasy in the bedroom.'

'Artez!' The shocked exclamation came from Cosima. 'Don't turn on Destine as if she were a tourist in search of thrills.'

'Oh, don't mind me, *señora.*' Destine gave Cosima a don't-care smile. 'I learned as quite a young nurse that men can be bullies, and the *señor* made it plain from the start that he regarded me as a dyed blonde who came to Spain in search of a Latin lover. He's so awfully Spanish that he's prejudiced against anyone who isn't a Latin born and bred.

83

He just doesn't like me, and I return the compliment.'

'Be that as it may,' he drawled, 'Nurse Chard will come with us on Sunday. That is what she is paid for, to be in attendance upon you, Cosima.'

And having spoken, and with the adamant look that warned he was not to be argued with, he strode to the archway that led from the room. Destine glared after him and she almost committed herself to saying that she wouldn't be here on Sunday, that she intended to leave this household that was so much under his dominance. The words were actually trembling on her lips when he paused beneath the archway and shot a look straight into her eyes.

'Contrary to what I expected, you are doing a good job, nurse. One has only to look at Cosima to see that you are weaning her off so many sleeping pills.' His glance moved to his cousin. '*Buenas noches, guapa*. Sleep well!'

He stepped beyond the archway and the door of the apartment closed decisively. Cosima drew her underlip between her teeth as she looked at Destine, and her eyes were amused. 'I know what you are thinking,' she said.

'You Latin people seem adept at reading the thoughts of others.' Destine drew the shoes off the helpless feet that felt cold to her touch. She began to massage them for her patient. 'And what am I thinking, *señora*?'

'That my cousin is an arrogant devil, and a moment ago you would have liked to have flung the words back in his teeth.'

'It was a great temptation,' Destine admitted. 'I – I can honestly say that I've never met anyone quite like him. He presumes to make judgments about other people, but he's no angel himself. He's impatient, intolerant and insular. Unless a woman is Latin, then lord help her!'

'He may have his reasons for being that way – as we all have reasons for being happy or sad.' Cosima drew off the clear sapphire ring that she always wore during the daytime, and Destine fetched the captivating antique box in which Cosima kept her jewellery. A small fortune in gems glittered and gleamed in the trays of the box, but they couldn't buy back for Cosima the freedom of movement and the caresses of Miguel Arandas for which she pined.

She lay back against her pillows with a sigh, and regarded Destine in the lamplight, her face pensive against the dark spread of her hair. 'If only I might change places with you,' she said. 'You aren't at all rich, are you, nurse? You have only your salary, and I pay more for my shoes than you can afford to pay for an evening dress. You are poor in everything but your health and freedom, and because you have those you are better off than I am.'

'It may seem so, *señora*, but you must take into account the fact that I have no family to care about me. I have no one, apart from my godmother, and back in England I have often felt intolerably lonely.'

'Then why do you insist that you won't marry again? The way out of loneliness for most women is to get into a man's arms, and you are good-looking enough to attract a man of means. There's Señor Davidson – he's a bachelor, and tonight he obviously found your company to his liking.'

Destine tightened her lips as she assisted Cosima out of her dress, and then pressed the bell beside the bed so that Anaya would come from the servants' sitting-room to prepare her mistress for bed. Destine was always careful not to offend the Spanish maid by taking over any of her personal duties, such as Cosima's beauty rituals, and the care of her clothes.

Miguel Arandas never seemed to be far out of Cosima's thoughts, and the reason she cared for her skin and her person was that she hoped against hope that her errant husband would come back to her. It seemed to Destine a forlorn hope, for had he loved Cosima he would never have left her when she so needed him.

'There aren't all that many good men in the world,'

Destine said, a slight edge to her voice. 'I'd never find another man like Matt – like my husband. I'd sooner stay alone than risk being unhappy with someone less kind, less good and clever than the man I lost.'

'If I could have Miguel,' Cosima said fiercely, 'then I wouldn't care if he beat me, so long as he was there, to be touched, to be seen, to be heard. To be hurt by him is not the hell – the hell is being without him.'

Anaya arrived just then, and Destine was relieved to see her. Cosima didn't talk so personally in front of her maid, and when Destine left the bedroom, Cosima was talking about sending for a new skin preparation which she had seen advertised in a magazine. She rarely opened a book and was an avid reader of magazines, unlike Destine who much preferred a good novel to the reams of advertising and lifeless fiction contained in the glossies.

Destine paused in the hall, where the wall lamps cast those curious, almost oriental shadows on to the pale walls. She supposed that it would be only courteous to go back into the *salita* to say goodnight to the company there, and yet she hesitated. She was, after all, only a nurse employed by the family . . . very likely she had not even been missed.

On impulse she turned in the opposite direction and made for the tall, wrought-iron gate that led outdoors, giving access to one of the side patios. The opening of the gate made no sound, as it was well oiled, and she stepped out into the night that was still and lovely and scented by bitter-orange blossoms and the breath of heaven that hung upon the walls of the patio. Petals and leaves rustled in a soft breeze, and fireflies darted among the trees. Overhead in the velvety denseness of the sky the stars were points of pale flame, quivering with a beauty far out of reach as Destine wandered to a low stone wall and sat there, alone and wrapped in a transitory sense of peace.

Her conversation with Cosima drifted back and forth

across her mind. It was a blessing to have good health and be able to walk in a garden and know that you were not dependent upon the tolerance and patience of other people. Poor Cosima, lying there in her elegantly draped fourposter with her jewels in a box beside her. Depending on Destine and unaware that her brother had been responsible for the death of Destine's bridegroom.

There had been no time for any loving . . . no memories of a real marriage, only a few lines on a document to ever show that she had been a wife at all.

Her fingers played with some orange blossom which had fallen from the boughs on which the fruit was also growing. Nurses from the hospital had thrown paper blossom over Matt and herself; there had been laughter and the usual jests when they had driven away from their wedding breakfast, heading for their honeymoon in Cornwall . . . heading for grief instead of joy.

Tragedy struck so swiftly, and yet ever afterwards it had an effect on your life. It was like a note of sad music that never quite died away; it was a small blank space in the heart that nothing could fill. It was an anger and a pain, and here at the House of the Grilles she was close to all the forces which had led so inevitably to that fatal car crash.

Here had Manolito been born . . . here in this very patio he must have played as a child, and perhaps later on kissed the women in his restless life.

Leaves rustled and Destine shivered as the night air touched her skin through the lace of her blouse. Like all old houses it was a house of ghosts and she swiftly turned her head, sensing a presence, and she couldn't suppress a gasp as she caught sight of the white glimmer there beneath the tree-bougainvillaea that arched over the patio. A hand leapt to her throat as she felt the frantic beat of her heart.

'Be easy,' said a voice. 'You were on the verge of a scream.'

She was powerless to reply, or to move. It was as if his silent approach had turned her to stone. Those eyes that were so densely dark that the pupils were lost in them were upon her upraised face, only faintly revealed by the patio lamp in its stone niche, flickering in and out of the faintly moving leaves.

'You walk like an animal,' she gasped. 'Are you following me?'

'For what reason would I follow you?' His tone of voice was ultra-mocking, and yet Destine caught the flash of fiery arrogance in his eyes and she was reminded that he not only resembled Manolito but there were the same passions and drives in his blood, and unlikely to be satisfied by what he felt for Cosima.

'You are either trying to drive me away from Xanas, or you are trying to find out if I – I can be made love to.' Destine leapt to her her feet, for now she had found the courage to delve into what so disturbed her whenever she found herself alone with this man. She was a nurse and she was no fool ... she knew that sensual attraction could flare into life between a man and a woman who were otherwise antagonistic. It was the very opposite of love, but it could be equally potent, and she was afraid.

Afraid of what she might feel if he should touch her.

'It would be unnatural if you and I, a woman and a man strange to each other and yet living under the same roof, were not aware of one another. Hate is as shattering an emotion as love, *señora*, and you do hate me, don't you?'

'Yes,' she breathed, knowing that her hatred had its roots in the way he made her feel, awake again to that physical self she had fiercely denied since Matt had died, in pain like a frozen limb upon which the ice was melting. She hadn't wanted to feel so aware of a man ever again least of all someone who was the dark, living shade of her husband's killer.

As a fury of rejection rose in her, she wanted to claw and

bite him, like a young animal; rake cruelly the scarred face, hurt him for being so vitally, so mockingly alive when the man she loved was no more, his ashes scattered from the cliffs of Helzion where they would have been lovers.

With emotion choking her, she turned away from him and clutched at a limb of the bougainvillaea tree. The heavy, beguiling scents of the night were all around her, alone with this man whom she rejected with every atom of her body.

A cry broke on her lips as his hand wrapped itself about her neck as if it were a stem he could break. 'No one,' he said with cruel distinctness, 'can live with the dead. Certainly not you, for if you can hate me so that you actually burn and tremble with it, then you are alive and not half buried with someone who can never look at you again, and feel your skin against his fingertips.'

'Let me go!' In the instant that she wrenched away from him, he did let go of her neck, for his fingers were strong enough to have broken it. But at the same time he hooked his other arm about her body and swung her against him, locking her to his lean hard body with the frightening ease of someone who had handled horses all his life and never debilitated an athletic body in the pursuit of idle pleasures.

'*Let me go*!' The panic in her voice was more intense, and her eyes were blazing as she flung back her head and looked up into his face. 'I hate your touch – it's like something devilish!'

'Like my face, eh?' He crushed her to him so that she had to look at him. Relentlessly he forced her to see each aspect of his face that had been so badly burned in his youth, so that for all time it would be painful for any woman to look at him. The flames had destroyed certain facial muscles and the scar distorted his left eyelid and made him seem forever mocking.

'If you stay here, then you will see me often, *señora*. There is no way that we can avoid each other, and no way that we can deny that a certain spark of unholy attraction takes fire when we are alone like this. Neither of us wanted it to be this way. I would prefer that you leave, and you may be sorry if you stay.'

She shivered as he held her with strong hands that had been so gentle with Cosima. Yes, it might well be lethal to her peace of mind if she stayed within his aura, yet what true peace had she known back in England? There was no sense of peace or security since Matt had died, and she felt a sudden recklessness as she faced the Don. He endangered her body, but he couldn't touch the heart that she had buried in a quiet grave with Matt.

'I—I can't leave now I've taken on the care of your cousin,' she said. 'It wouldn't be fair to her now we've become accustomed to each other. I—I'm not afraid of you, Don Cicatrice. You can't use your face and your threats to make a trembling fool of me.'

'Yet you do tremble,' he murmured, and his eyes were darkly wicked as they dwelt on her upraised face, with the fair hair framing her very English features. 'I can feel those tremors running through your body like the finely strung wires in a fine instrument wound up too tightly. You must take the advice that you no doubt give to Cosima—you must learn to relax.'

'With you around?' she retorted, before she could control the words that admitted how much he disturbed her. 'I know you, *señor*—you'll deliberately set out to make this job uncomfortable for me. It will be a means of amusement for you.'

'You think I am so taxed to find amusement that I shall prey on you whenever the opportunity offers?' He gave a mocking laugh, and then he held her away from him and flicked his eyes up and down her slender figure. 'If you ride, Nurse, then you might be distracting company—I have several young horses that are always in need of proper

90

exercise, and one in particular, a spirited filly, might be an excellent mount for you. What do you say?'

'I do ride,' she admitted. 'A hospital I worked at was close to a park and I took lessons, but I don't know that I'd be able to handle your horses.'

'Afraid of taking a fall?' He stared at her, and she seemed to read in his eyes a double meaning in his words. She felt the nervous throb of her heart and wanted to jerk her wrists from the grip of his fingers.

'Each time we speak, *señor,* you seem to be taunting me as a woman, as a nurse—someone who has a mind and a will of her own. Before you met me, were women merely compliant to your will, or scared of your scar? I don't plan to be either of those things, for I've seen scars before, and hospital consultants can be almighty arrogant!'

'So now I'm arrogant, eh?'

'You know better than I what you are. You have lived with yourself long enough to be acquainted with your own ways, *señor.*'

'If I am arrogant, then you are an impertinent chit of an English girl.' His fingers tightened on the bones of her wrists until she thought he would break them. 'Is that painful, Nurse?'

'Yes,' she gasped. 'What are you doing—?'

'Finding out if you have good wrists. My horses are mettlesome, but I think you might handle Madrigal quite well, and if you are determined to remain at the *casa,* then you must have a horse of your own. The estate is a large one and the best way to see it all is to ride over the place.'

'Madrigal,' she murmured. 'What a lovely name for a horse.'

'It means a love song.' And with a swiftness that shocked the breath from her lips, the Don had hold of her by the elbows and he was swinging her over the waist-high wall upon which she had been seated. He leapt in her wake and

91

walked her in the direction of the stables, made unmistakable by the aroma of horses and hay. They walked into the yard and along the length of stalls with their dutch doors closed for the night. About midway along the stables he paused and unlatched one of the doors, swinging open its upper part. A nearby wall lantern shone its light into the stall, and Destine saw a sleek, honey-coloured horse with its head bent to a trough of oats, which it was chewing with a lazy enjoyment, only pausing a moment to cock an eye at the couple who interrupted supper in this way.

'This is the filly which you will ride.' The lantern light shone on the unmarred profile of the Don, and Destine briefly noticed the hard, coin chiselling as she returned her gaze to the horse. 'Well, Nurse, what do you think of her?'

'She's beautiful, but she looks full of spirit.'

'Yes, but she has a good mouth and takes to a good rider. Well, do you think you could ride Madrigal?'

'I'll try. It's good of you, *señor,* to offer one of your best mounts to a novice.'

'Only by riding a good mount will you become an excellent rider.' He closed the dutch door and they walked back along the stone paving of the yard, while overhead Destine saw that the stars flirted with the sky, and she could hear the leaves of trees whispering as she and the Don made their way through the garden. He was a strange, unpredictable man, and she didn't want to be softened in any way by a gesture of kindness from him. Not that she really believed that he was being kind. He knew how isolated was this region, and if she intended to go on caring for his cousin Cosima, then she would need some outlet, some means of enjoyment when her patient rested.

They came to the archway that led into the *casa,* and she gave a start of renewed alarm when he stepped in front of her and she was forced to stand still. Hating that sense of surprise that could almost throw her off balance, she spoke

92

involuntarily. 'What is it, *señor*? Must I show my gratitude in more than verbal thanks?'

'Would you like to?' he drawled, and his eyes were glittering down at her, that signal of danger there at the centre of the jet-dark pupils.

'No – ' she stepped back and away from him and found herself against the stone of the archway, with his tall figure barring her escape from his mockery and her own foolhardy words. In all her time as a nurse she had never been so tempestuous, so unguarded, and she just had to find a way to get back at him for so unsettling her.

'You're the last man on earth I should like to kiss of my own free will,' she said, trying to ignore the fact that her body was trying to do the impossible by shrinking into the stone against which he had her trapped. 'Oh, don't imagine that I'm afraid of you – I just don't like men who assert their masculinity and regard women as mere ornaments and objects of male pleasure. I imagine that women and horses mean much the same to you, and I'm quite sure that if I were fat and forty you wouldn't dream of offering me one of your lovely horses to ride.'

'Indeed not,' he said, a smile thinning his mouth into a dangerous line. 'If you were fat and forty, then I'd offer you one of the stable mares with a nice broad rump. So that is what you think, eh? That I am a male chauvinist who believes that women should be seen but not heard? Well, in many respects that attitude has its advantages, especially when a woman chooses to put words into my mouth.'

'What do you mean by that?' Destine demanded, colour sweeping into her cheeks at the way he looked at her, as sure of his own strength as she was uncertain of hers. Nothing – no slings and arrows of angry words could ever alter the fact that he was a man and she a woman, with the physical superiority always on his side. Struggle as she might, they both knew that he would kiss her if he felt

93

inclined to do so and nothing she could do would stop him.

'It was you who said that I was asking for more than verbal thanks—the thought didn't enter my head, Nurse.'

'I don't believe you,' she exclaimed. 'Men always want something from a woman for anything they give—I've only ever known one man who wasn't selfish in this way. Other men just take all they can get, and they aren't interested if a woman isn't prepared to divide herself into little snacks for all and sundry. A blonde nurse, they think, is sure to be silly and willing. She must know all the answers because of the work she does. Men still seem to associate nurses with the type who did the work before Florence Nightingale came along and made the profession a respectable one. When you met me at the railway station you were quick to let me know what you thought of me, and now that I've agreed to continue with the nursing of Cosima, you've decided that you might as well take advantage of the English nurse.'

'Is that what you really believe?' He moved a menacing step closer to her, a dark Spaniard of the south whom she had dared to challenge. A man unaccustomed to having his motives questioned by a mere woman. A man still very much unknown to Destine, who felt her heart beating fast beneath the lace of her blouse as she strained away from him.

'Y-you wouldn't bother with me if I weren't young and fairly attractive,' she said, striving to keep her voice more controlled than her leaping nerves.

'Come, don't be so modest.' His hand moved and his fingers encircled her throat, holding her so that she had no way of avoiding his eyes. 'You are much more than attractive, Nurse. You are, I believe, what is referred to as an English rose—and you also have the thorns to prove it! What a thorny young creature you are, to be sure. This man you married must indeed have been brave, or was he the kind who only wanted the rose and not the woman?'

'Oh—how dare you say that!' Destine glared at the Don,

feeling the touch of his hand on her throat, sending little darts of fury through her system. 'I – I could kill you for that!'

'My dear, it takes cold blood, not warm, to go through with a killing, and I can feel the warmth of your skin against my fingertips. You know, if you are going to hate every man for being alive while your husband lies dead, then your life is going to be one long trauma. One day you are going to love again – '

'No,' she denied, shaking her head so that her hair escaped the calot and fell around his fingers. 'Matt was my ideal, and I shall never – never want to love again.'

'Yet you will,' he said inexorably. 'It will be a different kind of love – perhaps a more vital and tempestuous emotion than the one which a young girl feels for the first man who enters her life. The very young are inclined to make idols and heroes of those who touch the untried heart, but now you are a woman. You have suffered – '

'Oh, I'm glad you realise that, *señor*,' she broke in. 'I was under the impression that you regarded me as a dizzy blonde – '

'Now you speak nonsense.' His voice cut into her. 'You are clutching at straws so that I won't talk about what the future might hold for you. You want to go on living in the past, because it is safe, and it gives you an excuse to cling to a dead man. A live one might wake you up to desire – he might make you forget the young surgeon who treated you as if you were made of spun glass.'

'How do you know how Matthew treated me?' She glared up into the dark face that was so different from the image that she carried in her mind of the man who had been her husband for six unfulfilled hours. 'You know nothing of his kind of love – you would treat a woman as your total possession, and her life would be dominated by you. She would be a wife only, and heaven help her if she wanted to have a career, or pursue any other activity, for that matter.'

'I admit to being wholly Spanish when it comes to a wife,' he drawled, and he made a shiver run through Destine as he deliberately stroked his fingertips across the skin of her throat. Her head reared back as if to escape his touch, and he smiled narrowly at her inability to escape him. 'What is wrong with a man wanting a woman who will devote herself heart and soul to him?'

'It's an arrogant, outdated assumption that women are meant to be tied to the belt and buckle of the man they marry. In England marriage has become a civilized arrangement, and if a wife wishes to work, then the husband gives his blessing and they form a working unit—'

'And live on tinned peas and frozen fishcakes, eh?'

'One would expect you to be sarcastic about it,' she retorted. 'The Moorish blood in your veins would be bound to make modern marriage seem too free and easy. You are the type who would like to see the harem and the purdah brought back into fashion. While women are kept in submission it makes your sort feel high and mighty—but women aren't slaves! They're human beings and entitled to share in all the rights and privileges that men have enjoyed all these years. It was their determined selfishness that kept women from really fulfilling themselves.'

'And are you fulfilled, *señora?*' His gaze held hers, quizzical, faintly amused, as if all her brave talk had brushed off him and left him quite unconvinced by it. 'And please spare me the insistence that you have your career, for I can't see the pleasure for any woman in being constantly in the presence of pain and fear.'

'Someone has to do the nursing,' she protested. 'Someone has to care for the sick—'

'Yes, but not exclusively. Not for always. Not you, Destine, and shall I prove it?'

'No—just let me go!' Her heart was pounding, and she

96

Keep your free copy of this special "Collector's Edition"...

Please answer the simple questions on the card, detach and mail today. We'll be happy to send you this special "Collector's Edition" of *Lucifer's Angel* by Violet Winspear absolutely free. It's our way of saying "Thank you" for helping us publish more of the kind of books you like to read.

LUCIFER'S ANGEL

One of the classic romance novels by this world-renowned author! You'll enjoy reading Violet Winspear's explosive story of the fast-moving hard-living world of Hollywood in the '50s. It's an unforgettable tale of an innocent young girl who meets and marries a dynamic but ruthless movie producer. It's a gripping novel combining excitement, intrigue, mystery and romance.

Newly printed in a special "Collector's Edition"! We've published a brand new "Collector's Edition" of Violet Winspear's first Harlequin novel. And a complimentary copy is waiting for you. Just fill out the card and mail today.

knew that he must feel the pulse in her throat that kept time with her heartbeats. 'I – I have to look in on Cosima to see that she is comfortable, and I'm tired – a nurse, you know, is on her feet a good deal of the time.'

'Is she?' he said, and the next moment, with that agile strength that always took her by surprise, he swept her up into his arms and carried her beneath the archway, into the hall of the *casa*, striding with unimpaired ease along the arcades, where the wall-lamps threw their saffron light in and out of his dark eyes.

'Please, señor!' she gasped, clenching his shoulder. 'Put me down at once – before someone sees us! Whatever will they think? Please – I insist – '

'You see,' he mocked, 'for all your independent talk, and your insistence that you're an emancipated career woman, you have no way of getting out of my arms unless I choose to release you. You are at my mercy, Nurse!'

'You – you're just exerting your brute strength – your bullying instinct – '

'Not my gallantry?' he asked tauntingly. 'Not my concern that my cousin has had you waiting upon her since early this morning? You really give me no credit for a single act of kindness, do you?'

'You aren't being kind – you're being impudent and mocking, just to teach me a lesson because I dared to argue with your egotistical ideas. You aren't used to it, and so I have to be shown that I'm a weak female without your muscles!'

'Praise be!' He laughed in his throat as he dropped Destine lightly to her feet, just short of Cosima's apartment. 'Very well, Nurse, I let you go if you promise to take a swift look at Cosima and then go off to your own bed. I will give your farewells to the Marquesa's guests – unless you wish to say a personal goodnight to Señor Davidson?'

Destine looked into those ironical eyes bent upon her, and

97

once again her fingers itched to land a slap against his sardonic cheek. He was just about the most infuriating devil she had ever met, and it seemed an impossible feat to try and get even with him.

'It's a relief to be saying goodnight to you,' she said. 'May I hope that you'll leave me alone in future, now that you know that I'm not the free and easy sort?'

'*Señora,*' he drawled, 'had you been easy of virtue, then it would have been all too easy to disregard you. *Buenas noches* Nurse Chard, and do sleep undisturbed.'

'I intend to, *señor,* if you're hoping that I shall be disturbed by anything you've said to me. Goodnight!' She swept open the double doors and entered her patient's sitting-room without looking again at Don Cicatrice.

She felt she had made a good exit, but she couldn't ignore the unsettling effect of certain things he had said—nor could she brush away the lingering feel of his hard fingertips against the skin of her throat. Her skin tightened, tingled, and made her feel curiously guilty as she approached the bedside of her patient. It came as a stab of relief that Cosima was sleeping, for it wasn't until she was right beside the bed that she realised the tousled state of her hair. Had Cosima been awake to see her, she would have wanted to know why her nurse was so unusually discomposed.

Destine lifted a hand to her hair, and her hand was unsteady.

CHAPTER FIVE

THE mornings at the House of the Grilles were always a source of amazed delight to Destine; one of the compensations for working here in the deep south, so far from home and acquaintances, among people whose star of tragedy had crossed with her own.

It was no exaggeration to say that the sky was clear blue as a gem, with the sun catching the leaf-tips of the palms and a pair of giant fig trees. Near the cane patio table where Destine sat awaiting her breakfast there was a sheer, living screen of golden allamanda, and when she glanced in the opposite direction there were quince bushes with shell-like flowers, huge oleanders of white edged with wine, cascading creepers heavy with scent and some flamboyant velvety red flowers into which the bees flew in and out, carrying gold pollen on their wings.

Here she chose to start her day, drinking in all the loveliness and peace of this secluded, mosaic-paved *carmen* before proceeding to the bedroom of her patient.

She listened to the persistent droning of sounds, a mingling of chirps and chortles from the treetops, underlined by the humming of the many hidden cicadas, the very voice of southern Spain, it seemed to her. From morning to dusk they could be heard, so there was never any real silence around the *casa*. Even when the birds were still, the cicadas could still be heard, and it was a sound that had a curiously soothing effect upon the nerves, for as the maid came to the table with the breakfast tray Destine didn't give that start which had been apt to annoy her before she became used to the agile, almost catlike way these Latin people moved about their business.

'*Buenos dias, señora.*' The young maid gave that usual wondering smile as she rested her eyes on Destine's sunlit hair. The sun made it seem even more glistening and fair, especially first thing of a morning when Destine left it loose about her neck. Always before going in to Cosima she rolled it at her nape and pinned it, but for this hour that belonged exclusively to her, she allowed herself to be less prim and proper.

'*Buenos dias*, Imelda. Isn't it a stunning morning? I do believe this is almost my favourite time of the day, though I must admit that your Spanish sunsets are breathtaking.'

'The *señora* grows to like our country?' The maid arranged the breakfast dishes on the table, the sunlight glinting on the silver domes as she removed them from the plate of ham; thick, home-cured slices fried like bacon, with sliced tomatoes and rounds of crisp potato at the side. There were also ring-shaped rolls fresh from the oven, and *cafe bueno* – rich dark coffee such as Destine hadn't tasted until she came to this part of Spain.

Everything that came to the table of the Obregon family came from their own estate; they were, Destine had discovered, as self-sufficient as their feudal forebears had been – apart from the modern amenity of gasolene, and she felt sure that if Don Cicatrice had ever found oil on the family land he would have gone ahead and drilled for it.

He was, in every way, the modern equivalent of one of those self-sufficient overlords of long ago, the reins of every branch of the estate held firmly in his lean, strong hands; his superlative guidance as undeniable as the skill of the knife in the hand of a surgeon.

Destine glanced about her and had to admit that she had grown to like certain aspects of a place she had expected to hate every minute of the day.

Though the *casa* was haunted for her, it also had a kind of magic that was surely in its walls and trees and intricate lacings of iron and had nothing to do with the Obregons. People came, and people went, but a house had a life of its own, and so she could say to the young maid in all sincerity that she had, indeed, grown to like her surroundings.

'They are quite unique,' she murmured. 'I – I believe I'm glad now that I came to Xanas. It is a fabulous place.'

'But very quiet, *señora*.' The maid sighed. 'Sometimes I feel I should like to go and work in Madrid – do you think I would like it there? My mother says that it has become a fast place.'

'Oh, it's certainly a lot different from Xanas,' Destine agreed. 'Very busy and overcrowded – I think, Imelda, that you might be overwhelmed by the traffic and the more modern pace of life after the beauty and spaciousness of this region. I'm sure I shall notice the difference when I return to all that.'

'You will be going soon, *señora*. Like the other nurses? They, too, found it very quiet here.'

'No, the quietness doesn't bother me, but one day the Señora Arandas will be much improved in health and I shall move on to another nursing position – this really is delicious coffee, Imelda. One thing is certain, I shall be a coffee addict before I leave the *casa*.'

'I am glad you are not yet leaving.' The girl smiled shyly. 'You are not like the other nurses, for they complained much of the time – I think because the Señor Don was a little too haughty and did not unbend to their smiles. Cook says that nurses always hope to make the rich marriage and that is why some of them work in private houses.'

'Well, that isn't true of me,' Destine protested. 'I don't think I try to make the Señor Don unbend to me! I'm truly not interested in him or his wealth.'

'You fear his face?' Imelda murmured, with a glance over her shoulder. 'I feel a shiver when he looks at me, for he seems to have the face of two men, one handsome, and the

101

other so sinister. But some girls care only about money and they wouldn't mind his looks –'

'I don't care to discuss the Don or his looks,' Destine broke in. 'You had best be careful if you do so in the kitchen quarters, for one day he may catch you discussing him.'

'The saints protect me!' The girl swiftly crossed herself and hurried away, leaving Destine with a rueful smile on her lips. For an instant a sort of pity had stabbed at her – had his face not been ruined by that searing scar, then Don Cicatrice would have been a very striking man. As it was he did produce a kind of terror in a woman when he looked directly at her, the destroyed half of his face in conjunction with the well-marked brow and jawbone of the other side, ruled over by the proud Arab nose.

Oh, he knew his effect on women, she thought, as she ate delicious ham with a crisp slice of potato. He knew he either frightened them, or produced a sense of fascination, based on the fact that there were women who were drawn to the devil. Destine felt sure that even if fire hadn't marred him, he would still have been something of a devil ... it lay in his genes, in his stars, for he was first cousin to Manolito de Obregon, and Destine could never forget it.

She had almost finished breakfast and was eating a nectarine when she had a premonition of not being alone any more. She endured the feeling for about half a minute, and then glanced over her shoulder to where that great curtain of creepers lay glimmering and scented in the gathering heat of the sun.

Though with her every tiny nerve she knew who stood there, treading as silently as a great cat, it still came as a shock to her nerves when she actually saw the Don. In black, narrow-fitting trousers and a black silk sweater he looked like a panther standing there, dangerously supple and unpredictable. In an instant, like fine glass, Destine's sense of peace was shattered.

'I've never known anyone but a cat to walk so silently,' she threw at him. 'You aren't exactly good for the nerves, *señor*.'

'Well, *señora*, if your nerves are that bad, then I shall take to whistling a tune when I am likely to come upon you.' He strolled across the mosaic tiling, and very deliberately he whistled the *corrida* theme from *Carmen*, until he stood above Destine and could look down upon her fair, untied hair. 'What now, Nurse? Are you going to leap to your feet and announce that duty calls?'

'It does, *señor* – '

At once he glanced at the leather-strapped watch on his left wrist; the leather only shades darker than his skin. 'I estimate that you have fifteen minutes before your breakfast hour is concluded – I see that you have been enjoying a nectarine. Would you like to see the fruit trees in bloom with fruit and blossom? Come!' He reached for her hand and drew her to her feet, and because she wore her flat-heeled nursing shoes she felt very aware of his tallness. In that single respect he took after his Australian antecedents; in every other way he was entirely Latin. His skin, hair and litheness of frame were as Spanish as the sun overhead, and under his skin he was imperious and not to be denied by a female of the species.

'I am proud of our orchards,' he said crisply. 'They are like no fruit gardens that you will see in England, for the valley is protected by the mountains and our sun is undiluted by that coolness in your British atmosphere. A coolness that gets into the system, eh, as the golden warmth of Xanas gets into the bloodstream of southern-born Spaniards.'

Destine didn't argue with him, but she was acutely aware of his warm grip on her elbow as he led her from the *carmen* into the depths of the garden where she had not yet ventured. As it was still so early there were spider-webs glistening on the shrubs, silvery traps for any unwary fly on the wing. The very air had a sparkle to it, and Destine could smell the fruit on the heavily laden trees before they stepped through a wrought-iron gate that had interworked into its iron the name and crest of the Obregon family.

She gazed in wonder at the regular rows of trees, billowing with blossom, and with the globes and bunches of fruit there on the branches in the midst of the blossom. The Don was right, for nowhere in England could she hope to see anything as rich and lovely as this. The very sun had got into the fruit, so that the oranges, the nectarines, the peaches and apricots glowed with a honeyed ripeness. Their fruity musk hung on the air like a wine, and deep breaths of such air seemed to go to her head so that she felt half intoxicated.

But it was when they reached the lemon and grapefruit section that she really gasped; the citrus scents mingled and it was like no perfume she had ever breathed before.

'Wonderful, eh?' The Don looked at her, his eyes gleaming through his dark lashes. 'The trees bridal and bountiful at one and the same time, so in love with the sun that they give of themselves in this rampant fashion.'

'The very air is like champagne,' she agreed. 'I suppose the valley bottles it in?'

'Exactly so, and at this hour in the morning it is uncorked a little, so that it goes to the head – even to mine, and I am fairly accustomed to the orchards. You must feel, *señora*, as if you have taken a deep gulp of wine.'

'I believe I do feel slightly intoxicated.' She glanced at him and felt her heart give a quick nervous beat at the way his eyes were wandering over her; she became aware of how alone they were, here among the fruit trees, with only the birds and the bees in carefree flight around them.

She was unaware of the flush beneath her skin, and the way her brown eyelashes intensified the blue of her eyes in the frame of her silvery-gold hair. Her lips were a little open as she looked at him, still agleam from the rich juice of the nectarine, and she wore an open-throated blue silk shirt and a cream-coloured skirt that, on her, was very becoming.

'You look very young this morning,' he said abruptly. 'You should always wear your hair in that style, for it is less severe than the one I usually see.'

'I—have to be neat and efficient, *señor*. I am a nurse, remember.'

'But first and foremost a woman.' The sardonic look crept back into his eyes. 'So it is only when you are alone, taking your solitary breakfast, that you permit yourself to look the girl that you still are, despite the ring on your hand and the slab of marble on your heart. As the *dueño* here, I should insist that you keep to the un-bunned hair and the short skirt that shows your legs. Englishwomen have that advantage over the women of several other nations, they have most attractive legs—ah, now you look at me with the sharp nurse-eyes that demand that I be reprimanded for being so personal.'

He smiled narrowly and reached up a lazy brown arm for a lemon that hung just above his dark head. He plucked it, complete with a sprig of blossom, and deliberately handed it to Destine. 'A man with my face must not pay compliments, eh, nor give to a young widow anything sweeter than a bitter fruit? Despite my devil face I am but a man, and despite your widowhood you are but a woman, and if you wish to hide that womanhood you shouldn't match your eyes to a blue silk shirt, and reveal slim legs in a skirt to your knees. Take instead to the black shawl of the Latin widow—'

'If you think,' she gasped, 'that I am dressed to lead you on—! I didn't give you a thought until you dragged me here to look at your fruit trees. I was quite happy to be alone, minding my own business, and now you have the audacity to suggest—'

'No, *señora,* merely the audacity to admire you in much the same way as I admire these fruit trees. I suppose that even an ugly man may be permitted to do that?'

105

Destine bit her lip and looked away from him. She didn't think him ugly, only tough-fibred, with something of the barbarian only an inch or so under that sun-darkened skin of his. Her fingers gripped the lemon he had given her, which would be bitter, for there was still a tinge of green in its skin.

Had she grown bitter because of the waste of a man like Matt, so that all the old sweet joy of life had been squeezed from her heart, as this lemon could be squeezed so that only the skin and pith were left to be thrown away ... was she throwing herself away among the medicine bottles and the sterile white sheets of hospital beds? Oh, surely not, for Matt had loved her dedication to her nursing career and had wanted her to go on to higher things.

She tilted her chin and said, seriously: 'You and I, *señor*, could never agree about anything fundamental. You think that a woman's sole aim in life should be to please a man, but I dress to please myself, and I run my life on the same principle.'

'And were those principles your guide-light, even when you married your doctor, Nurse?'

'Yes – why not?' She flung a look at Don Cicatrice, who looked so flagrantly male standing among the citrus fruits and their tangy blossom. 'Matt was a civilized man – he didn't expect me to be dedicated to him alone. He understood that a woman needs to express herself beyond the confines of the home – oh, what is the use of saying it all again? You are far too Spanish, *señor*, to ever understand Matt or me. Your world is here in this valley. Your devotion is to the earth and what it yields. You don't care deeply about people – you'd only care if you could make them as perfect as your trees, growing lovely and silent out of the soil and obedient to your hand only. But a woman isn't a tree, made only to bloom and give.'

'You think not?' His eyes swept her from head to foot. It

would be fascinating to prove you wrong, but right now duty calls both of us and that little lesson will have to be set aside until we find ourselves alone again. I warn you –'

'And I warn you, Don Cicatrice,' Destine tautened in her every nerve and fibre, braced against his scrutiny and his daring strength. 'I don't want any lessons in female humility from you. Save them for your Latin ladies who appreciate male arrogance rather more than I do!'

So saying she swung away from him and uncaring that it looked like flight, she ran from him among the lanes of trees until she reached the iron gate. She took hold of it and was shocked to find that it was too high and heavy for her to move, so that she was obliged to stand there and wait for him to thrust it open with a single movement of his hand.

She flung him a look through a flying wing of her hair, and a mixture of emotions were there in her eyes – resentment, flight, and excitement. She could feel her pulses pounding, and as she ran on to the *casa* she felt a tingling aliveness and awareness of the sunlit morning, the blue clarity of the sky, and the warm brush of the sun on her skin. She didn't want to associate these sensations with the Don, but she knew very well that he had somehow lit her to this new aliveness. He had sparked her to this vivacity, which was still showing in her eyes when she hurried in to her patient, having quickly changed her blue shirt and pale skirt for something more sober, and having bunched her hair into a hasty chignon.

'*Buenos dias, señora,*' she said breathlessly. 'I must apologise for being late, but I was – detained.'

'Good morning.' Cosima stared at Destine over her coffee cup, as if noticing that aura of added vitality. 'And by whom were you detained – you look as if it might have been someone who has put you on your toes?'

Directly Cosima said this, Destine realised that she had best not mention Don Cicatrice. Cosima was jealous of his attentions, and Destine certainly didn't want her to think there was anything going on between herself and that high-handed infuriating Spaniard who had a way of imposing himself upon a woman – even one who didn't particularly like him.

'Oh – I laddered my tights on a rose bush and had to change into another pair,' she said, telling what was only a white lie, for she had ruined a perfectly new pair of tights in her flight from the Don, and if there was one thing she hated it was to be seen going about her duties with a ladder running up her leg.

'Really,' said Cosima, and still she studied Destine as she applied almond honey to a crisp roll. 'Have you put rouge on your cheeks, or is that a natural flush to your skin? I suppose you've been dashing up and down that long flight of stairs! How I envy you, with your slim and energetic legs. You make me feel like a poor old lady.'

'Nonsense,' said Destine, and she set busily about her routine for the day and directed the conversation into a different channel. An hour later she had settled Cosima comfortably in her long chair on her patio, with magazines on the table beside her, her small radio, some fruit and biscuits. Since she had weaned her patient off so many sleeping-pills, Cosima's appetite had improved and the contours of her face seemed to be filling out.

With a little sigh, and her glistening dark head at rest against a silk cushion, Cosima regarded the blue and gold of the sky through the shielding branches of a tulip tree.

'And what do you think of Xanas?' she asked suddenly. 'I know it didn't appeal to you when you first came, but what are your feelings now? Are you more, or less, enchanted?'

Destine ran her glance over the tulip-like flowers that balanced upon the branches of the tree like so many pink candles, lit by the sun. She looked at the pastel water-lotus

108

floating in the alabaster bowl of the fountain that filled the air with its cool water music. Clumps of flowers mingled their scents, and the white kitten with the black tail dashed back and forth across the tiles in pursuit of the green lizards.

'I sometimes wonder, *señora*, if I am having a sort of dream when I look around me and find myself not in the austere surroundings of an English hospital, but in a gracious Spanish house. You've known it all your life, so you can't imagine how it strikes me. I sometimes have to touch a flower-hung wall, or an iron grille, to make sure they are real and not figments of a dream.'

'Yes,' Cosima looked interested by Destine's remark, 'I was born here and I am so accustomed to the place that I don't truly notice how unusual and picturesque the *casa* must seem to a stranger – one who takes the trouble to notice the house as a classic example of Latin–Moresque architecture. Have you done any exploring? We have a fine old chapel, with a bell-tower that has a story of its own to tell. Long ago a reluctant bride was married in the chapel, and so aloof and unloving did she find her Obregon bridegroom that when the ceremony was complete she broke from his side and gathering up her long silk skirts she raced up the spiral stairs of the tower and there threatened to throw herself from the balcony if he should attempt to touch her.'

Cosima paused and bit delicately into a cream biscuit, while Destine pictured the scene, and felt unsurprised that a girl should flee from a male of this family. She felt that each succeeding male must be in some way intimidating, and the girl had probably come from a convent to be married to a man she barely knew.

'And what happened, *señora*?' she asked. 'I hope the girl didn't carry out her threat.'

'No.' Cosima smiled a little and shook her head. 'Her bridegroom left her there and returned to the *casa* with his guests. He knew that sooner or later a girl so young, from

109

the convent schoolroom almost, would soon become hungry and then she would forget her dramatics and climb down of her own accord. The Obregon men are realists rather than romantics, as you have probably gathered for yourself. That wily ancestor of mine was fully aware that if the girl really wished to be free of him, she would have made her dash for freedom before the marriage service was concluded. He was a man of the world and he knew that he made her nervous – the story goes that he was waiting outside the chapel when she finally climbed down from the bell-tower, and he had with him a slice of the wedding cake and a glass of wine. His suave patience must have been rewarded, for they had three daughters, and a son to carry on the name.

'However,' Cosima frowned and plucked with a polished fingernail at the Spanish lace shawl covering her knees, 'nothing goes truly well for any member of this family. That particular ancestor was killed a week after his son was born. One of the plantation workers went berserk and struck at him with a cane-cutter, so you can see, Destine, that a sort of dark cloud does hang over this family and it seems as if nothing will ever disperse it. Perhaps we are punished for old cruelties, eh? No one can deny that there is a dash of cruelty in our bones – I am cruel to Madre when I speak of not wanting to get better. And my brother Manolito had a side to him that I tried to ignore – he was so very good-looking, you see. So dashing and daring and fearless. But we all knew – '

Cosima shrugged her elegant shoulders and looked directly at Destine, as if something of her tension had communicated itself. 'How you absorb my every word,' she said. 'Are you *that* interested in the history of the Obregons?'

'Y-you are an unusual family,' Destine replied, and her fingers were clenched together behind her and she was fighting for some control over her own feelings with regard

110

to Manolito de Obregon. His dark, rakingly handsome face was forever printed upon her mind; the face of a reckless pleasure-seeker, to whom danger would always have been an aperitif.

'Yes,' Cosima murmured, 'we all knew that Manolito was capable of inflicting pain. When he and Artez were boys, each one was given a colt of shining black, perfectly matched in limb and speed. And then one day my cousin beat my brother in a race they had staged, and that same night Artez caught Manolito in the stables, deliberately laming his colt with a riding-stick. Artez snatched the stick and beat Manolito about the shoulders with it, then he broke it and flung away the pieces, for he was always physically strong. I don't think Manolito ever forgave him for the humiliation of that beating, for it was witnessed by the stable workers. My brother was the *señorito*, you see, and Artez only a cousin who was kept by my parents. He didn't really have any money of his own until he came into quite a fortune when a relative of his grandmother's died out in Australia and left him well provided for.

'Ah, how I am talking this morning!' Cosima gave a slight laugh.

'It's good to hear you, *señora*.' Destine fought to speak naturally, for she felt deeply shaken by the things Cosima had talked about. 'It proves that you are getting better and regaining an interest in people.'

'Indeed it does,' said a deep voice. 'You are breaking out of your apathy, *cara*.'

Don Cicatrice had stepped through the delicate iron gate that gave access to the patio and for a moment he stood outlined against the dark iron in which were twined the scarlet flowers of a climbing geranium. The sun fell upon him unrestrained, and yet it had the curious effect of veiling his scar a moment before he moved, so that Destine's hand flew to her throat, stifling a cry. So absorbed had she been in

111

Cosima's revelations that the Don had seemed to appear as Manolito . . . a shudder ran all through her. How alike they would have been, until the facial likeness was burned away in a stable fire.

Cosima must also have seen that momentary likeness, for she said, as the Don took her hand and bent over it: 'You quite startled me, cousin. We were talking of Manolito, and there are times when you – '

'I know,' he said, and as he kissed her fingers, he slanted a glance at Destine. It seemed only a glance, and yet he probed into her eyes as if curious about her reaction to Cosima's conversation. He had warned her never to speak of her connection with Manolito, for he wouldn't have those he loved hurt again by the old wounds. That his cousin's name could always hurt her was immaterial to him. She was no part of him as Cosima was, and the Marquesa who had been like a mother to him. He did not spread the net of his affections wide and freely, but those he gathered in would always be sure of his protection.

It gave Destine a bleak feeling as she watched the Don lean over Cosima and brush with his lips the pale and elegant fingers. It came to her with sudden sharpness that she had had to face her own grief and pain in great loneliness; there had been no strong hand held out to pull her through. She had cried in the darkness all alone . . . and suddenly here in the sunlight the tears seemed to sting her eyes and she looked quickly away, in case those quick Spanish eyes should see the sudden wetness that she blinked rapidly from her eyelids.

All at once Cosima gave a low trill of laughter. 'I think, *caro*, that we embarrass my nurse. The English are not *simpatico* with our foreign demonstration of affection and prefer kisses to be exchanged in private. You see how she turns her head away from us – is it shyness or is it envy, do you think?'

'I would say that it is neither,' drawled the Don, and a

112

quiver seemed to go across Destine's face, and she swung round and spoke to Cosima in a tense voice:

'I am sure I don't wish to be *de trop*. I'll go and tidy the bedroom, *señora*.'

'But you aren't a housemaid,' Cosima rejoined, and her eyes glimmered darkly as she swept a glance over Destine's face, which try as she might couldn't help but express the emotional tension that she was feeling. 'No, I wish you to stay and be decorative, for it isn't often that the Señor Don has the opportunity to see a young woman who has legs that move and aren't pieces of dead wood like mine. He's very gallant, of course, but an invalid is really a bore to a man – '

'You are never that, Cosima,' he objected. 'There is more to a woman than an active pair of legs.'

'Is there, *caro*?' Cosima's smile was moody. 'Are you trying to convince me that you prefer my passive company to that of someone who can walk at your side, ride with you across the land, and feel you holding her from her heels to the nape of her neck? If so, cousin, then you had better become a monk.'

He laughed shortly and leaning forward drew a finger down Cosima's pensive cheek. 'Come, snap out of this. A while ago you were talking with animation, and now you are being self-pitying. Look at the sky, *cara*, look at the flowers and hear the birds. Life is good for anyone who has eyes to see, and ears to hear. There are always compensations, *mia cara*. Life is always better than the lonely darkness of death.'

'And believe me, cousin, the sky is always bluer and the flowers always sweeter if one sees them in the company of one's lover. You speak of compensations – what truly are mine, Artez? I can never be a wife again – unless you are offering yourself as a husband?'

With incredible distinctness the words rang out in the patio, and Destine found that she was looking at the Don

113

rather than at the woman who flung at him these provocative words. Not a feature of his strong, scarred face betrayed surprise or dismay.

'If, Cosima, it will make you happy to be my wife, then I will certainly marry you.' His words were equally distinct, and there wasn't a shadow of doubt in Destine's mind that they were as binding to him, in that moment, as if spoken in the chapel.

'When the divorce is final, eh?' Cosima drew a sigh. 'Miguel will divorce me, out there in California, and I don't blame him. I never have blamed him for leaving me – he isn't like you, *caro*. He isn't strong and self-sufficient – he has none of the old *conquistadore* spirit in him that enables men to suffer all kinds of torment. Madre would be over-joyed if you and I made a marriage, and I really believe you would endure a wife who could never be a total companion to you. You would make that sacrifice for me – ?'

'Yes,' he agreed, taking both her hands and holding them so they were lost in his. 'I think, Cosima, that we belong together, you and I.'

'Do we?' She gazed up into his intent face, and it struck Destine that she was intruding on a very private moment. She had almost reached the arched glass doors that led into Cosima's apartment when her patient called out to her:

'Don't go, Destine, before you congratulate Don Cicatrice and myself. You have just heard him propose to me, so do be the first to wish us joy of each other.'

Destine turned slowly from the glass doors and a shaft of sunlight gilded her hair as she stood there, but shielded the exact expression in her blue eyes.

'Congratulations, *señora – señor*. I hope you will both be happy.'

'But do you approve?' Cosima insisted. 'Do you think that a new marriage will make a new woman of me?'

Several emotions struggled within Destine, for she had not

spent days and nights with Cosima without learning that she still cared for Miguel Arandas. If Cosima married the Don, then she would do so out of defiance and the need to prove that she could still make a man want her. Destine had no way of gauging the Don's feelings, for though he was looking at her, his eyes were unreadable and his face was a marred copper mask.

'The very best medicine you could have, *señora*,' she said, 'is the serene contentment of knowing you are cared for.'

'What a very charming way of putting it,' said Cosima. 'I must now float through life like oil on the surface of the turbulent waters, eh? Will it suit you, Artez, to be the serene *novio*?'

'I want only your happiness,' he said. 'Ah, and now I think of it! We are due to go to the *finca* of our friends tomorrow, and we will be taking Nurse Chard so that she might have another *tête-à-tête* with Señor Davidson. You will come with us, of course?' he flung at Destine.

'Very well,' she spoke politely. 'If you insist, *señor*.'

'Don't make it seem like a chore,' he chided her. 'You will enjoy seeing a little more of Xanas.'

'If you say so, *señor* – '

'Not to mention the good-looking Welshman. Celts can be very striking, can't they, Nurse?'

'Can they, *señor*?' Destine gave him a wide-eyed look of innocence. 'I really wouldn't know, devoted as I am to my nursing duties.' With this parting shot she slipped in through the glass doors and swiftly and neatly closed them behind her. Once out of range of the patio she felt she could breathe more easily – heavens, how these Spanish people could take one's breath away! Walking from the sitting-room into the bedroom she caught sight of herself in the mirror that fronted the ceiling-high clothes closet, and she paused and stared at her face, which had the look of a shock which had not yet worn off.

115

What had shocked her? The fact that she had heard Cosima and the Don pledge themselves to each other? But why should she be shocked? It was an open secret that he cared for Cosima, so it ought to be the most natural outcome that he should eventually marry her and heal the hurts that Miguel Arandas had inflicted.

Destine stared into her own intense blue eyes ... she felt strangely off balance, as if she wanted to go and sit quietly by herself until that shaky feeling subsided, and those odd nerves stopped twisting and turning inside her. But the entire incident had been so unexpected, and she just couldn't convince herself that those two could ever be truly happy together. The Don was so – so vital, so much a part of the land, as the rocks and trees and mountain eagles were part of it. But Cosima was delicate and cosseted, like an indoor orchid that must never feel the full force of the elements.

Destine moved about the exquisite bedroom, and the tidying up she had talked about had merely been an excuse to get away from those two, out there making their plans for the future. Here in this room were the kind of things that lay close to Cosima's heart, the pleasure in the beautiful *estrellon* above her bed; the rose window that shafted jewel colours on to the pale walls and ivory-silk trappings of the fourposter. Alpaca rugs of a creamy whiteness lay across the floor, and captivating, expensive little frivolities stood about on small tables.

It took almost all of Destine's imagination to try and visualise the Don in this bedroom, dark and towering, his fearsome scar reflected back and forth in the big, mother-of-pearl framed mirrors.

Destine's hand shook slightly at the mental image and she almost dropped a small white china shoe that looked as if it might have come off a wedding-cake.

She turned the little shoe about in her fingers and instinct told her that the shoe was off the big, shining white cake that

Cosima had cut with Miguel Arandas by her side, glowing and lovely in her bridal dress, breathless with joy, and so unaware that her joy was to be so short-lived.

Destine replaced the shoe very carefully on the little table beside the day-bed between the long windows. She stood there looking out upon flowering trees that arched in the sunshine, so laden were their branches with a satiny red flower. For some people happiness was like a flower, so splendid for a while, and then a cluster of dying memories. No, she thought, Cosima wouldn't reach out any more for a glamorous love, much as she pined for it. She had looked at last at her powerful cousin and seen there a refuge for her stricken body. She had looked at his face and decided that no other woman would ever really love him, and it was part of the Latin soul to clutch at *saudade* if real romantic joy was not to be had.

That afternoon, while Cosima took her siesta, Destine took advantage for the first time of the sleek riding horse which the Don had put at her disposal. In breeches and boots which Cosima had insisted that she borrow, she went down to the stables and went along to the stall in which Madrigal was standing, her handsome head poking out of the open section of the dutch door.

Destine entered the stall with a slight feeling of nervousness, for she and Madrigal had to become friends as soon as possible, and though the horse jibbed when Destine started to saddle her up, she quietened down at the bribe of a sugarcube and allowed herself to be led out on to the cobbles of the yard, towards the mounting block, where Destine climbed into the saddle with just a little trepidation. Back in England, at the riding-school near where she had worked, the mounts at the disposal of the pupils had not been as highly bred as this young Spanish horse, with its glossy coat, pricked ears and plume of a tail.

With a fast beating heart Destine directed the horse out

of the gateway of the stableyard, and along the well-tramped path that led towards a range of open country, gradually inclining above the valley land where the orchards and the plantations had their fertile home. The air was alive with the rich perfumes of the valley, and the sun overhead had a hot, golden glow, which made Destine glad that she had taken Cosima's advice and put on the brown slouch hat that went with the fawn breeches and the silky sweater. The brim shaded her eyes but allowed her to enjoy her surroundings that had an indescribably wild and lonely appeal, just suited to her present mood.

In a while she and Madrigal had adapted to each other, so that she began to feel more confident and gave the lively horse a little more rein.

As they cantered higher in the hills, the valley below took on a shimmering green and gold look in the sunlight. Destine could feel her eyes shining, for there was no denying that back in England, tied always to the wards of various hospitals, she had had little chance to see anything as lovely, and exciting, as this. Here one could breathe and feel the pulse of rampant life, enclosed from the rest of the world by a crest of distant violet-tinged mountains. They had the sheer beauty and terror of a stronghold that could not be invaded by the modern world of fast cars and faster lives.

Here some of the barbaric splendour of the past still lingered, where white-walled villages lay for this golden hour in a slumbrous quiet on the hillsides, their streets arcaded, with narrow windows encased in iron grilles in which the thick stems of geraniums had long since become as tough as the iron, producing long trails of scarlet flowers that threw their shadows on to the crusted white walls. Hammered lanterns clung in ancient brackets beside the arched alleyways, and here the sun-glare was muted as Destine rode through them, feeling as if she had cantered through a time-curtain into another era, another century.

'Time is the servant not the master in Spain,' she thought, and her eyes dwelt on the various sized pots that were drying in the sun outside an old pottery works on the edge of the village. There was no sign of the potters, for siesta held sway over the place, creating a magical hush that would only be broken when the sun began to decline. Then, like busy ants, the people would reappear from behind their shutters and they would work, bargain and gossip until well after nine in the evening, by which time the air of the village would be rich with the aroma of spicy Spanish food. *Chilli con carne,* hot *churros,* and meat and onion *tortilla.*

Spaniards loved the night time. They ate late and talked far into the midnight hours. The afternoon siesta was their solace from their glorious but terrible sun and Destine smiled slightly as she and her mount broke the silence that prevailed, the well-shod hooves clopping on the flat-worn cobbles of the village street.

It was probably true, she thought idly, that the English were a little eccentric, for here she was, out in the sun while sensible Spaniards lolled beneath their bed-nets . . . or kissed in the lush and drowsy warmth.

Her fingers tightened unaware on the reins and Madrigal took this as a hint to break into a gallop through the twisting, narrow streets until they came out once again upon the hillside. Destine held hard with her knees, for Madrigal was not to be stopped now she had started to gallop, and there was fear mingled with exhilaration as Destine was carried higher and higher into the hills, the slouch hat blowing back on the cord that tied it and her hair romping loose about her flushed face. It was only when she saw a sheer plateau above them that she began to tug on the reins in an effort to slow down her mount. But the devil had got into the filly and she refused to obey the English girl who had replaced the young stablehands in her saddle.

When Destine realised that she was no longer the mistress

119

of the ride, her heart thumped and she had a wild vision of being flung from the saddle, down over the side of the plateau they were rapidly approaching.

She was indeed almost flung, for suddenly a piercing whistle cut the air, a zephyr of sound winging to the ears of the filly and causing her to stop almost dead in her tracks, so that Destine was jerked forward, her booted feet slipping free of the stirrups, her hands clutching wildly at Madrigal's mane in an effort to save herself.

As she lay in that undignified position she heard the sound of hooves behind her, pounding like her heart as they came closer, and a swift look around showed her who the rider was. It shot through her mind that he looked amused a moment before a frown drew his black brows together.

'Why did you whistle like that?' she gasped. 'You almost had me over Madrigal's head!'

'Your mount was out of control,' he thundered, riding up beside her and looming dark against the sunlit sky, and so arrogantly in control of his own horse, whose coat had the sheen of mahogany, the silvery bridle rattling to the toss of its handsome head. The Don's hands were firm on the reins and his breeched knees were close in against the muscular sides of the animal.

Destine struggled into a sitting position, while Madrigal stood there so sedately, pretending she had not taken advantage of the female stranger.

'You are miles from the *casa*.' The Don swept a critical look over her tossed hair and the hat that lay against her nape, the cord across her throat. 'I suppose you realise that had you been thrown, and hurt, it might have taken hours for me or my men to find you. Until you become more used to handling a high-spirited horse you should have kept within a mile or so of the *casa*, for Madrigal knows she has lighter hands upon her reins and she was bound to misbehave. Nothing Spanish is easily tamed, *señora*.'

'So it would seem.' Destine now held her mount's reins more firmly, and felt as if his riding-whip had curled across her skin. 'I saw the houses of a village and I just had to explore, and then Madrigal got a whiff of the hilly air and she was away. I suppose everything of yours is trained to obey your whistle?'

'You will admit that it sometimes has its advantages.' He pointed with his whip to the plateau that ended in a sheer drop to the rocks. 'It's better to be alive than to lie a bundle of bones down there, would you not say?'

Destine gave a shudder and thought how graphic was his language at times. He rarely minced his words into small, easily swallowed morsels, and obviously had no time for the complimentary language of the Latins she had met in Madrid, mainly at the house of her godmother. Was it the Australian blood in him that made him less smooth, or was it the jagged scar that made him ... different?

'Tell me, *señor*, do you admire the paintings of El Greco?' She asked the question impulsively, and felt the raking of his narrowed eyes as he considered it.

'By that, *señora*, do you mean do I prefer what is stark and real to what is veiled and romantic?'

'I – suppose I do mean that.' And yet even as she spoke Destine wasn't sure what she really meant ... unless she felt that the scarring of his face had somehow scarred his true self.

'Then you must have forgotten that I have a dash of the desert in me,' he said, 'as we all have, here in the south where the Moorish overlords had their courts and their favourites of the veil. It would go a little against the grain if I didn't have an eye for beauty, even as the beast had, eh?'

'Don't – talk like that –' Yet involuntarily her eyes were upon his scar and instinct told her that there might have been a girl who had shrunk from him because of it, someone other than Cosima, for Destine could never believe that he

121

felt a passionate response towards his cousin. Protective, yes, but there were fires in this man which Cosima had never aroused, even when she had been fit and lively, and able to ride and dance.

'This is very stark and real, isn't it?' He placed the shaft of his whip against his face. 'The woman who lives with me will have this to look at night and day, but Cosima is accustomed to it. She was a small girl when it happened and she accepts it – enough to be my wife.'

'Is that why you're marrying her?' The words had a will of their own and Destine heard herself speak them, horrified. She stared at the whip in his hand and felt that he might strike her with it, for she had no right to pry, and hated people who did so.

'I don't need to tell you my reason for marrying any woman,' he said cuttingly. 'You are the English nurse at the *casa*, nothing more, with no lasting place in our lives. You have come, and you will go, and together Cosima and I might find that serenity you spoke about. But I am not marrying her because my face is acceptable to her, and that is all you need to know. What is close to my skin, and beneath it, is not for you to get at, and if you have some idea that Cosima is turning to me for consolation rather than romance, then let it be admitted. Let her turn to me rather than turn her face to the wall and be locked away in her memories. "One broken dream is not the end of dreaming", so they say. "Still build your castles, though your castles fall".'

'Of course.' Destine had a strange sense of bleakness as she looked past him to where the mountains had their keeps and their turrets high in the sky, and she could almost wish that he had lashed at her with his whip rather than his words. They left their sting across her mind, so that on the ride back to the *casa* she kept remembering them.

The dazzling sunlight was on the wane as they came in

122

sight of the valley, above which the sky was now like a painted ceiling, glowing with heavenly colours. A richly fragrant stillness overhung the plantations as the heat of the day began to die, bringing out the mingling scents of cane and tobacco; coffee and fruit.

The Don slowed his horse and Destine followed suit, her eyes shielded by the brim of her hat as she took a quick look at him. He was gazing downwards, and his nostrils were tensed to that bouquet, as if for him it was more exciting, more poignant, than any perfume worn by a woman against her warm skin.

'Land is to a Spaniard what *sal* is to a woman,' he said, and his voice had deepened with the day so that his words seemed to be a purring sound in his brown throat. 'Good yielding land has almost the same quality as a woman's charm—or would you, with your clinical training, accept that as an unflattering description?'

'Coming from a Spaniard it seems appropriate, for I expect he believes that only plenty of tilling and drilling will produce a willing woman.'

'Willing?' He gave a rough sort of laugh. 'The best of earth is never willing, but has to be coaxed and fondled and treated to the best of food and dressing. Here in Spain that is particularly so, for our sun is an enemy as well as a friend, and we have to be constantly attentive to the land if it is to give of its heart and not merely its topsoil. It has taken years for this valley to be as it is right now, but that perfect abundance would soon wither away if for one single day any part of it was neglected. It is a full-time occupation, apart from this siesta hour, when like you, *señora,* I go madly out in the sun. This is my world and I rarely, these days, go beyond those mountains. I have here all that I ask, and that must seem very insular to a modern young woman.'

'No,' she said, surprising herself, she so rarely agreed with this man. 'If a person has found the right job, in the right

123

place, then it seems only restless if he should wish to be in other places all the time. I really don't believe that modern life is perfect – I've never said that.'

'It is only modern marriage that is perfect, eh?' He glanced down at her, and his eyes glimmered mockingly in the dark angles of his face.

'At least preferable to the Latin arrangement,' she argued. 'But as you say, the Spaniard does seem to place his land and his horse ahead of his woman.'

'Is that how it seems to you?' he asked drily. 'I thought we Latins had a romantic reputation abroad, and that everyone believed us to be veritable Don Juans, with nothing else to do but dally beneath a balcony with a guitar and a rose in the teeth. But now you inform me that we Spaniards are not the great lovers; that the *loco amor* takes third place with us.'

'With you, I think, *señor*.' Destine gestured at the valley, which in the deepening dusk had almost a violet tinge to it. 'Would you exchange all that for a woman? I doubt it!'

She spoke so definitely that a deep, short laugh broke from him. 'She would have to be some woman,' he drawled. 'I have put most of my adult life into that valley; skill, sweat and pain, and I should, indeed, have to be mad with love if I turned my back on the plantations in order to follow a fickle beckoning finger. I agree with you! No woman is worth all that!'

With this he swung his horse away from the valley in the direction of the *casa*, and as they cantered along the track that led to the stables, night dropped its cloak and a sudden feeling of coldness made Destine shiver.

'Go along indoors,' he said, when they had dismounted. 'I will see to the horses – and, *señora*, next time you ride, don't go so far from the *casa*. Not until you are more accustomed to Madrigal, who has a strain of Arab in her.'

'Like her master?' Destine quipped, and she hastened

124

away before he could make a retort, entering the hall just as the Marquesa came out of her daughter's apartment.

'Nurse – just the person I wished to see!' Cosima's mother was smiling as she approached Destine. 'I have just had a little talk with Cosima and she has given me some wonderful news. She and Artez have decided to marry when that Arandas man releases her from what was never a true marriage. I am so very happy! I have wanted this for so long and now my daughter at last has the good sense to want it also. After dinner tonight we must open a bottle of champagne to celebrate!'

As she said this, so joyfully, the Marquesa caught at Destine's hands. 'I do believe, my dear, that you have brought good luck into our house, for it is only since you came that Cosima has brightened up, and now she tells me this most happy news, that she has accepted a proposal of marriage from Artez. Did you know of this?'

'Yes – I knew.' Destine smiled, but she was thinking to herself that it had been Cosima who had proposed the marriage. They had been speaking of compensations, and she had challenged him to be hers ... in the form of a husband.

'It will be good for Cosima, eh?' The Marquesa pressed her rings into Destine's fingers, and now her fine eyes held a suggestion of tears. 'It will make up for what she has suffered, don't you agree?'

'Of course,' said Destine, while vividly across her mind rode a tall vital figure on a horse whose coat seemed darkly aflame beneath the setting sun.

No one asked ... no one thought to ask if such a marriage would be good for Don Cicatrice. It seemed to be accepted that a man so scarred couldn't be expected to want a radiantly eager bride ... a girl who could look at him and not flinch from that cruel disfigurement.

'They are meant for each other,' said the Marquesa, and

the pressure of her rings had become a pain that Destine endured in silence. 'Like unto like.'

A wild protest ran through Destine, but she kept it to herself. What right had she to speak in defence of a man who had said that she was but the nurse here ... someone who came for a while ... someone who would depart, leaving these people to find what happiness they could in the House of the Grilles.

Window grilles were ornamental iron bars, and bars a prison made.

the pressure of her rings had become a pain that Destine endured in silence. Like until the A wild protest ran b but she kept a c....

CHAPTER SIX

THE sun was glittering across the courtyard and catching like points of diamonds in the water falling from basin to basin of the Moorish fountain, and Destine stood beside the car, watching as the Don carried his cousin from the *casa* and brought her to the big open-top tourer in which they were to drive to the *finca* of the Spanish family with whom Lugh Davidson was staying during his sojourn in the south.

Cosima had dressed with great care, and her make-up was exquisite, but all the same she looked fragile and almost childlike in the strong arms that lowered her carefully into the car on to the embroidered linen seat-covers. 'There,' he said. 'You are comfortable, *carissima*?'

'I – think so.' Cosima held on to his arm as Destine settled a cushion behind the frail spine, then she settled back and smiled at both of them, liking the attention and aware that she was looking lovely, with her dark hair smoothed into silk under the wide brim of a white hat, her dress a deep rose-pink that went so well with the Latin complexion. Her eyes flicked up and down the figure of Destine, who had chosen to wear a simple blue dress with a trimming of white around the collar and cuffs. It was cool and she had felt that such a dress would emphasise the fact that she was Cosima's nurse and not a guest in any way.

'How very English you look against our Spanish background,' said Cosima, and a polished fingernail gleamed against her dress as she adjusted one of the silky folds. 'I think if you lived in Spain a dozen years, Destine, you would still continue to look as if you had just stepped out of an English dairy.'

'How very bovine you make me sound, *señora*.' Destine

127

smiled, but she was intensely aware of the dark, almost stern gaze of Don Cicatrice, and a start ran all through her as he suddenly gripped her elbow and assisted her into the car beside Cosima, on the wide back seat. She still felt his touch as he slid into the seat in front of the wheel, and for an instant her eyes were fixed upon his iron-firm shoulders, covered by the pale fawn material of his well-cut suit, so perfectly tailored that she was aware of strength without seeing a hint of bulging muscle. Then she quickly averted her gaze to where the Marquesa stood beneath a myrtle-laden archway to watch them drive away. She looked a little sad, a little lonely, but had declined to come with them, insistent that Cosima enjoy her outing without her anxious mother in attendance. After all, Cosima had her *novio* in charge of her, and he would ensure that no harm came to her. Words that had seemed weighted with the implication that had he always been her chosen consort then not even polio would have dared to lay its cruel hand upon her.

Cosima waved to her mother, and they drove off under the great archway of the *casa* and continued through the property for at least a couple of miles before turning on to the main highway. Cosima threw various remarks to her cousin about the countryside and how unchanging everything was, while Destine sat quietly there, with apparent composure, and let her thoughts play with that first journey she had taken along this road, not in a large, smooth-engined car, but in that old-fashioned vehicle with the sound of hoofbeats on the road, breaking into the silence of the night.

A tiny smile of irony tugged at her lips. She had thought the Don the chauffeur, which was ridiculous in retrospect, for in his impeccable fawn suit he looked every inch the *hidalgo* that he was. And oh, how he had set her temper on edge – and still could, with a look or a remark that was meant to make an opponent of her.

Yes, if she stayed here a dozen years she would still be

very English, and still she would find the Latin temperament as complex as a Moorish arabesque. No matter how hard you looked at such an arabesque, it seemed forever impossible to see where it began and where it ended.

'You are very quiet, Nurse Chard.' The deep masculine voice broke in abruptly upon her thoughts. 'Are you overtaken with admiration of our southern landscape? Those blue tips of the mountains, those strange rocks sculptured into shape by the sun and the wind, that shimmering sunlight, and the chalky-jade cactus? Ah, glance to your left and you will see the romantic ruin of a Moorish castle! That should appeal to your vivid imagination, and underline what you said to me about the men of the south and their attitude towards women.'

'Ah, this sounds intriguing.' Cosima played her eyes over Destine, who was glancing back at the slim sun-peeled tower that dominated a heap of broken stones where long ago a Moorish lord had housed his soldiers and his slaves. 'What have you been saying to Artez that seems to have impressed him so much?'

'I'm sure, *señora*, that nothing I have said could really impress the *señor*.' Destine spoke lightly, ever aware that her patient was jealous of any attention not directly given to her. 'I am merely of the opinion that things of the past affect us in certain ways, and here in the deep south many things have remained unchanged – attitudes of mind, let us say.'

'And of the body, let us add.' Cosima flicked a look at the smooth dark head of the man in front of them. 'So you think that Artez still inclines towards the seclusion of women in preference to letting them lead a liberated life. You are right, of course.'

He gave his brief, dark laugh when he caught his cousin's remark, but he didn't bother to argue with it. 'Liberating a woman is like revealing a secret,' he drawled. 'Where there is no mystery there is no mystique.'

129

'Meaning you would like to see the pair of us in yashmaks?' Destine shot at him.

'Both of you in yashmaks would imply that I had a pair of women all to myself,' he rejoined dryly. 'Is it an implication you would enjoy, Nurse Chard?'

The shimmering temper came into Destine's eyes at the way he could turn her words to suit himself; playing with her as a tawny cat might play with a mouse. 'I wouldn't enjoy being the slavish plaything of any man, *señor*!'

'How can you be so sure, Nurse? The facts of life are like the facts of food – one must sometimes taste the dish before pronouncing it to one's liking.'

'One can often tell just by looking,' she said, and almost instantly regretted words that could mean only one thing – that having looked at his scarred face she had no liking for what she saw.

'Oh, do stop bickering, you two,' Cosima said in a bored voice. 'I have rarely known two people so opposed to each other. Like oil and water you will never mix, but for this one day do try to be amicable, even if you only pretend. It is my first social visit in a long while, and I've looked forward to it.'

Immediately Destine saw a relaxation in the Don's shoulders, as if at Cosima's appeal his entire mood softened. 'I promise you will have a good day, *cara*. The sun shines for you, and you are looking very attractive in that outfit which must have been bought in Paris at one of the most fashionable salons. You will outshine all the other woman at the *finca*.'

'You really think so?' A purr came into Cosima's voice, and as if to assure herself that the Don was paying her a sincere compliment she took her gold powder-box from her handbag and studied her face in the mirror. 'One thing I'll say for being an invalid, it does make one look thin and interesting. I hope I never get fat like that wife of Fernan-

130

do's! It's true she still has a pretty face, but her hips have pads of fat on them and her ankles have lost all their grace. Who would believe, looking at Susana now, that she was once a very good flamenco dancer? I would sooner go hungry than look as she does!'

'What does it matter, Cosima, when Fernando still very much loves her?' A dry note had come into the Don's voice. 'In the eyes of a lover a woman never really changes – unless she loses a sweet temper for a sour one.'

'I have never before heard you speak like that, Artez. *Mio caro*, when did you develop a liking for the placid temper in a woman? I have seen you polite to the various placid wives of our friends, but I have never seen you – fascinated by them. Just as I have never seen you ride a tame horse!'

Destine listened to this exchange with a tense interest that she didn't dare to question. What was she listening for? That note of love in the lover's voice? That breathless note of wonder in Cosima's voice? That unmistakable sign that these two were emotionally involved. Ah, she was being a romantic fool! Marriages were arranged every day in Spain, and nine times out of ten they worked out more satisfactorily than the ones that had love for their driving motive.

Half an hour later they had come in sight of the *finca*, with its grasslands where the bulls of Fernando Castros grew from rough-coated calves with comical horn-buds into sleek, strong animals that were sold to farmers for breeding purposes instead of the slaughter of the bullring.

There was a sound like thunder as a group of calves went galloping past the car, throwing clods of grass from beneath their hooves and making a primitive picture in the blazing sunlight over the *sabana*.

'One should be an artist – a painter in Spain,' Destine exclaimed. 'It must be the clarity of the atmosphere, and the mountains, that make such a picturesque background for every detail. It's like – like living in a vast canvas, with nothing modern or ugly to spoil the scenery; no concrete walls or plates of glass; no enormous container-lorries filled with chemicals; no sky clouded by factory chimneys.'

Then, a trifle embarrassed by her outburst, Destine gave a self-conscious little laugh. 'I must sound like the most naïve tourist on a coach outing, but I do find southern Spain very beautiful, and most unusual.'

'Beware, *señora,*' said the Don. 'To become enamoured of Spain can be a dangerous thing, for when she bites she holds on, and you have a career in England that must be pursued, have you not?'

'Yes,' she said clearly. 'But surely I can—like your country without finding myself—held, as you call it.'

'Like it by all means,' he said, 'but don't let the bite be so deep that when you wrench yourself away a part of you will be left behind. This has been known to happen, and despite your skill as a nurse, your status as a married woman, you have a certain—vulnerability. You were so busy with your career that you forgot to be a girl, but now in Spain the girl in you is let loose—' He turned a brief instant in his seat and his eyes swept her hair, loose and sunlit about her face. It was a look that imparted far more meaning than any words, and a slight flush came into Destine's cheeks. She wished instantly that she had secured her hair at the nape of her neck, and had kept to herself her swift admiration of this land that was so tawny and blue and closed off from the noisy streets where people fell beneath fast wheels and were brought into hospital like broken toys to be mended. Here there was a certain peace and glory to which she had responded, and now she was hurt, and ready to blame him for the dismal reminder that she was but a visitor and must remain so.

'Don't worry, *señor,*' she said distantly. 'I shan't outstay my welcome in your country. I am here to do a job of work, and when it's done I shall take my leave without being torn in two. That can only happen once, anyway – ' There she broke off, for she still felt hurt, still felt stunned that she could feel with an intensity she had believed had gone with Matt. She had made her work her life, but here in Spain a new set of emotions had grown over the grave of dead ones, and she was suddenly afraid of them and in almost a panic she took stock of the *finca* as the big car drove into the courtyard, where the sun lay dazzling on the thick white walls, the many different levels of windows and roofs, where the tiles were arched and ox-blood red.

She held her breath and then let it out. Again the pure, primitive beauty of something Latin had caught her heart in its fist, and she was lost, drowning in delight as she looked around her.

'No, nothing changes,' Cosima murmured. 'It's still as I remember it as a girl, when we came here to dance in the patio to the guitars of the gipsies. It hurts that nothing changes while I – I am altogether different. I can't dance any more, or run up to the balconies to throw roses at the young men. Oh, why did I come here? I am better at home, shut away from the old memories!'

'You came to enjoy a good day with old friends,' the Don said, kindly but firmly. 'Only cowards sit alone in dark rooms, spelling their memories like black beads, and you are no coward, *carissima*.'

'Circumstances make cravens of us,' she rejoined. 'Turn the car, take me home before – '

But it was too late, for with a gush of frilled dress and a laugh of welcome the plump and pretty wife of Fernando Castros had come running from an arched doorway. Her curvaceous arms were held out as if to embrace each occupant of the car, and her eyes were sparkling against the almost Moorish gold of her skin. She was a picture in herself, thought Destine. The adored mother of two boys and a girl, and quite obviously indulged by the dark-clad Spaniard who followed her across the courtyard at a more stately pace.

Beyond them Destine saw the tall figure of the Welshman and she felt a quick sense of relief that she wasn't going to be the only foreigner among all these Latins.

'*Mia cara*,' Susana reached for Cosima's hands and clasped them, 'how good it is to see you again at the *finca*! We had such good times, eh, and will have them once again, now that you are so much improved.'

'From the look of both of us,' Cosima swept her cynical look over Susana, 'I would say our dancing days are quite over, just as the old days are over. I merely called for a few minutes – we shan't be staying.'

'Of course we shall.' Don Cicatrice had stepped from the car and with that courteous firmness that wouldn't be denied he opened the door beside Cosima and placed his arms around her, lifting her with ease from her seat. 'Fernando, perhaps you will be so good as to get the wheelchair from the boot? Nurse Chard will show you how it opens and operates, for it is one of those new, light models that appears to run on magic.'

The magic was a concealed battery, and the chair itself had all the comfortable refinements that money could buy, not being unwieldy in any way and designed for self-control. But Destine knew that Cosima hated it, the outward sign that she couldn't use her slim legs and had to propel herself through life from now on.

Destine expected a tantrum at sight of the chair, but something in the Don's eyes, some secret pressure of his arms seemed to subdue his cousin and she permitted him to carry her to the chair. The laugh she gave was defiant. 'You see how masterful he is, Susana,' she cried. 'He gives me a demonstration of how he will be when we are married!'

The words seemed to stab through Destine, and she hoped her face betrayed no sign of stress when Lugh Davidson came to her side and she turned to greet him. Her hand felt lost in his warm clasp, and he didn't speak right away but studied her in silence, a sort of wonderment in his eyes at the fairness of her hair in the golden sunlight.

'I am never sure about women when I see them by the artificial lighting of a drawing-room,' he said at last. 'The sunlight can be terribly cruel to some women, but you are obviously one of Apollo's handmaidens.'

Destine smiled, unsurprised that a Welshman should speak with poetry in his voice. 'I'm pleased to see you as well, Mr. Davidson. I was rather daunted by the thought of being a lone Anglo-Saxon among a group of Spaniards – they can be rather overpowering, can't they?'

'Some of them,' he agreed. 'Don Cicatrice, for instance.' Lugh had drawn her to one side, so that they stood apart from the Spaniards, the group having been enlarged by the arrival from the house and stables of weekend guests and resident relatives. Cosima was the centre of the attention, with the Don towering over her, not saying much, but somehow not needing to speak to be noticeable.

'Did I hear correctly?' Lugh murmured. 'Did Cosima mention marriage, or was she indulging in a cynical jest?'

'There is a possibility that her husband will divorce her, and if so a marriage will take place between her and the Don.' Destine spoke with composure, but inwardly she was still very much shaken by her own reaction to each mention of the marriage. She couldn't pin down the source of her disquiet, she only felt that it was adding to the tragedy for such a union to take place. Cosima needed to be loved, not pitied, and Destine felt convinced that the Don had no passion in his bones for his invalid cousin.

'You don't quite approve, do you?' Lugh had caught the note of reserve in her voice. 'Are you a romantic, Destine? Do you live by your name, that destiny should bring two people together, and not the austere voice of duty or pity?'

135

'I think it a pity that her husband didn't stand by her,' Destine replied. 'I am sure she still loves him, and responds more to shallow charm and gaiety than to anything – deeper.'

'And in your estimation the scarred Don is deep waters, eh?'

'One look at the man is sufficient for that,' she half-gasped, and she didn't need to look to see him standing there, one hand at rest in a pocket of his fawn jacket, his mouth bold and just a little cruel, and above that slight smile on his lips the deeply slanting cheekbones, the proud arch of the nose, hawk-like, with an equally deep arching to the brows, his skin bronzed like Cordoban leather. That face had been close to hers and she had seen how deep were the oceans of his eyes, going down, down into primitive deeps where all women would be lost, but from which Cosima would be safely kept.

'Such a marriage could work,' Lugh murmured. 'It's bred in Latin bones to marry for family reasons, and there isn't much left for that poor girl but to be cared for and protected. Yes, he's a man who might be cruel, but not to her. You see that, don't you, you with your clear blue eyes?'

'Yes, I see that,' she agreed, and didn't add that she saw very little warmth in such an alliance – unless the Don saw the heritage of the *casa* and its lands secured for him by marriage to Cosima. Her heart jolted – ah yes, that could well be his real, true reason, for she had often thought that if he had any love to give, then he gave it to the miles of cane that rustled like a bamboo forest, and to the fruit yards rampant with scent in the valley. It was there, in the long hours, in the hot sun, that his skin had darkened to that saddle-tan, holding all those tangy aromas in his very pores.

God ... she pulled forcibly away from her own thoughts, feeling a sort of dizziness that made her clutch at Lugh Davidson's arm. 'Sorry ...'

136

'No, don't be.' He pressed her hand to his skin. 'I've been waiting a long time for someone like you to hold on to me –'

'No,' she pulled her hand away, for he had spoken too intensively to be flirting with her. 'I don't want – what I mean is that I wasn't touching you to start anything – physical between us. I'd like a friend, Lugh. That would be nice, but you'd find me ice-cool marble if you wanted to round out your Spanish visit with an affair. I just seem immune from all that boring, permissive feverishness.'

'Utterly immune, I'd say.' His smile was admiring as it dwelt on her. 'You're cool as the camellia, and what a lovely change that is from the brash and over-eager females crowding out the nice girls and making them feel freakish because they don't indulge in every form of licence. Nice has become a nasty word to the so-called moderns, hasn't it? And as for love – can they even spell it?'

'I doubt it.' But she didn't want to be drawn into a discussion of that complex and bewildering emotion; she didn't want to believe that she could ever feel again that need to belong to another person. 'I think we'd better join the others, don't you? They won't like it if we appear to be standoffish –'

'Or are you afraid that they might think we like each other's company a little too much?' He smiled down at her with eyes that were amused and also intrigued. 'I believe you're afraid to unlock your emotions, Destine. You no longer trust life to be kind to you, eh?'

'Can you blame me?' She started away from him, but he caught her wrist with his fingers, pulling her back among the clambering pink cameos. 'Lugh! We'll be noticed and they'll think – '

'Let them think it.' His voice had deepened and the hint of Celtic poetry seemed more insistent. 'You may be afraid of life, but I'm not going to believe that you're afraid of me, and I won't let you run away from me.'

137

'I have my patient to think about,' she said tensely. 'I want to make sure that she's all right – '

'Cosima is fine and enjoying being the centre of attention. Half her cure lay in facing up to life again, as you must.'

'Don't tell me what I must do!' Destine fought to release her wrist from Lugh's fingers. 'And don't make me conspicuous in front of these people or I shall dislike you. Please! I have my job to think about and I shall be dismissed if the Don thinks I'm playing about with you. You know how circumspect these Spaniards are with regard to their employees, and I'm only here today to keep an eye on Cosima. I'm not a guest as you are.'

'Nor is Don Cicatrice quite the dragon that you make out,' Lugh grinned. 'He's looking at us right now, but he isn't scowling and about to toss you out of the *finca* like a fallen woman.'

At Lugh's words Destine instinctively glanced in the Don's direction and her heart plunged when she caught his dark eyes upon her and Lugh, her wrist imprisoned in the Welshman's fingers, the pair of them against a background of wild pink roses.

It was true what Lugh said, the Don wasn't scowling but was regarding them with eyes so inscrutable that there was no telling if he was annoyed or totally incurious. He had lit a *cigarro* and he casually raised it to his lips as Destine jerked free of Lugh's grip. She felt a flush run across her cheekbones, for she so prized her own attitude of coolness and hated it that the Don had witnessed her slight tussle with Lugh.

Still feeling that unwelcome heat in her face, Destine strove for dignity as she walked to Cosima's chair, where she bent over the *señora* and quietly asked if she was comfortable.

'I'm fine, Nurse, so don't fuss.' Quite gone was Cosima's earlier look of panic and it seemed to please her to be playing the elegant invalid for her friends, who had clustered around her and were gaily laughing at her brave if slightly cynical witticisms.

'I highly recommend an English nurse if any of you fall and break a bone,' she drawled. 'Not only is my one pretty, but she is wise enough to let me eat chocolates in bed – after all, what else can I do there except read a book?'

There was a burst of laughter, and a few quizzical looks from the men at the tall figure of Don Cicatrice. He was taller than any of them, Destine noticed. Fernando Castros and his brother Sanchez were many times better looking in the true Latin tradition of sensuous brown eyes, well-shaped features and a smiling glint to the teeth. But handsome as they were they didn't compel the eyes, the thoughts, the curiosity as did the Don with his scarred face and his sardonic air of being of them and yet apart from them.

Cigarro smoke issued from his hawk-nose and that twist to his lip caused by his scar seemed deeply ironic as he caught those looks from men who had married active women who had given them sons as well as physical happiness.

Destine felt the beat of her heart, for in the face of all of them he seemed aloof, scornful, even dangerous. She felt that they were hornets buzzing against his tough skin. Nothing – no one could ever hurt this man as the elemental force of fire had. It had been a kind of *auto-da-fe* from which he had emerged with a lonely inner strength that was almost frightening.

'Destine!'

She gave a start as Cosima addressed her, that little hint of sharpness in her voice. 'You will be good enough to fetch my handbag from the car. I need my powder-case.'

'Right away, *señora*.'

Destine hastened to where the touring car was parked in the courtyard and she leaned over the side to where Cosima's hand-worked leather bag lay on the seat. Her fingers caught at the strap and then she gave a stifled gasp as she felt

139

her foot slipping on the step, only to catch her breath anew as she felt herself saved by a strong pair of hands.

Still holding her by the waist, they swung her around, but already she knew to whom the hands belonged and she had her face schooled into a polite mask, though she could do nothing about the flush which rose under her skin. Flushed, with her hair fallen forward over her left eye, she looked at him and muttered a word of thanks.

'Wouldn't it have been easier to have opened the car door?' he asked dryly. 'Women are like cats, they seem always to take the devious route and the way that will cause mischief for them. If you had fallen and struck yourself on these courtyard stones – ' He allowed silence to conclude his sentence, and Destine gave a little shiver. He had the gift of emphasis in his looks, his words, and his eyes. But it wasn't only his emphatic picture of her sprawled on the cobbles, it was the fact that he had followed her to the car that really unnerved her.

'The *señora* asked me to fetch her bag – it didn't need two of us,' she said, and she wished fervently that he'd remove his hands from her waist before they were noticed by one of Cosima's friends. That they were her friends rather than his had struck Destine right away; there would always be something about Don Cicatrice that would keep most people at arm's length, and it would therefore be noticeable if someone came upon them and saw him touching her.

'I wanted a word with you about Señor Davidson. He seemed to be annoying you.'

'No – of course he wasn't annoying me,' she denied. 'Why should he?'

'Why should he not?' The eyes that were so naturally dark, and made more so by the black lashes and brows, swept an explicit look over her face and her person. 'As an employee of the Marquesa you are in a position that places you above the unwanted attentions of even a house guest of the Castros family, unless I mistook what I saw for eagerness on your part rather than reluctance? There are women, I know, who find the chase more exciting than the capture, and perhaps I am mistaken and you wish this man to pursue you?'

'One way or the other, it's my affair,' she rejoined. 'I am an employee and not a guarded Spanish girl who needs a *dueño* to keep an eye on her. I can handle Mr. Davidson—'

'It didn't seem that way to me, but then again I don't profess to be an authority on British passions. He had hold of you and you were trying to get away, or leading him on.'

'And what if I were leading him on?' Destine felt a quiver of temper run through her that the Don should take it as his arrogant right to cross-examine her. 'Anything pertaining to my personal life is nothing to do with you—you have no more right to probe into that area than I have to ask you questions about your—your private life. Every minute of the day you act the Latin overlord, but I'm not one of your field workers—'

'No one ever suggested that you were.' His hands gripped and he gave her a sudden shake that made her little heart-pendant dance against the skin of her throat. 'But as a British young woman in a foreign country you are entitled to be protected from wolves, whether they be Latin or Welsh.'

'Oh—really!' Destine gave a scornful laugh. 'Mr. Davidson is far less of a wolf than you are, *señor*! Has it escaped your memory so soon that you dragged me into a corner and forced me to kiss you?'

'I see that it hasn't escaped your memory.' His eyes narrowed and fixed themselves upon the gold heart against her white skin. 'But I recall that I was very much provoked by you—is that what you were doing with Señor Davidson, provoking him?'

'Of course,' she said recklessly. 'It's all I live for in my spare moments, a form of revenge against all men who aren't the man I loved. As a Latin with a dash of the Moor you should understand all about the vendetta and how it can become the ruling passion of a person's life. I live to break men's hearts – '

'Yes,' he took her up, 'I think perhaps you do. Be careful someone doesn't break your heart, *señora*.'

'How can anyone break something already broken?' she asked. 'Now please allow me to take the *señora*'s handbag to her before she grows impatient and sends someone to investigate the delay. You know how she dislikes being kept waiting and I don't want her to be upset today. She has found the courage to come here, and that took quite a lot of resolve, you know. She's a vivacious person and it hasn't been easy for her to let her friends see her as an invalid.'

'You must be feeling pleased with yourself, Nurse, for you have accomplished what my aunt and I were beginning to think of as an impossible task. Will Cosima continue to improve, do you think?'

'I see no real reason for any setbacks, *señor*.' Destine spoke confidently. 'She has you to depend on in a capacity greater than any nurse can offer. Marriage is the best medicine she could possibly have.'

'Medicine?' He quirked an ironic eyebrow. 'Is that how you regard me, Nurse? A stringent dose of tonic straight out of the cabinet of cures? You don't find it romantic that after all these sad happenings Cosima and I should suddenly be swept together by the tides of – fate?'

He had briefly hesitated before that final word, and Destine wondered if he had meant to use a more evocative term, such as passion. She understood why he had paused and changed his mind. There could be no real, sweeping passion between him and the cousin whom fate had so cruelly injured, and Destine dragged her gaze away from his mouth that upon hers had been fiercely warm and urgent … lips that curled in this instance, baiting her.

142

'Don't be shy, Nurse, of being your usual candid self. What woman could feel romantic about a face such as mine, and we both know, don't we, that Cosima sees in me only a strong crutch to lean upon, and though she might love that weak fool who let her down, she knows that I shall be constant.'

'So you know –' Destine bit her lip. 'Don't you mind that Cosima still cares for him?'

'Not that much!' He clicked his fingers, and then his hand came suddenly towards Destine's hair and she thought he was going to touch her. Nerves tingled and she ducked to avoid his hand, and heard him mutter something in Spanish, rather savagely. 'To be so *emocionante* because I brush away a bee that might sting you,' he mocked. 'My skin is tough and I'm used to the bees from working in the orchards, but you have a very fine-textured skin and a sting would not only hurt you but mark you.'

'Oh – I didn't realise.' That tingling sensation had now reached the backs of her knees, as if bees had got under her skin and were tormenting her. What had got into her to make her react, as he said, so emotionally? It had to be the climate, for only a short while ago she had been in a tussle with Lugh Davidson ... but with him she hadn't felt this sense of danger and provocation. She *had* known that she could handle him, for at heart he was kind and predictable. But the Don was a different species of tiger ... when he purred it was no indication that he could be stroked.

Unable to stop herself, Destine cast a look at him from beneath her lashes ... he seemed to be smiling, but it was really only the twist of his scarred lip that gave the illusion of a smile. 'I – I really must be getting back to the *señora*,' she said. 'You're her *novio* and she's very Spanish and possessive, and I don't want her to think –'

'Exactly what, Nurse?' His query was the very essence of sardonic irony, as if her mind lay open like a book for his inspection. 'What don't you want Cosima to think?'

'You know I don't have to spell it out,' she rejoined, and the skin over her cheekbones seemed to burn again. 'She's an invalid, *señor,* and every woman who isn't is a potential enemy who might take her man from her a second time. I'd hate Cosima to think I'd do that to her. I've established a good relationship with her and I don't want to spoil it while I remain at the *casa* as her nurse. In all probability she'll be well enough for me to leave in a few weeks, especially now she has started to go out again and to associate with old friends. In no time at all she'll be almost her old self and I shall be redundant.'

'Redundant?' His brow quirked as his left hand slid away from her waist. 'Meaning dispensed with because no longer needed, eh? Where will you go when you leave us, Nurse?'

She considered his question, fingers twined in the handle of the leather bag that was weighty with all the cosmetics that Cosima carried around with her, as if no longer sure of her looks. 'I think I shall return to hospital work—it's less personal and one doesn't become quite so involved with a patient's emotional problems, being part of a team, just another nurse on day or night duty. A hospital is such a busy place that there just isn't time for—introspection.'

'Yes,' he agreed. 'If one keeps busy then the deep thoughts are kept at bay, aren't they, Nurse? There, you are quite free to hurry back to your patient. I am going round to the stables to compare Fernando's horses with my own. He brags that he has a stallion of pure Arabian blood stock, but *por Deus,* what is pure any more? It is like hoping to kick dust to find gold. *Hasta luego, señora.* My *novia* should not be too suspicious of you, for she believed I was on my way to the stables to see this four-legged paragon when I waylaid you instead. She's as confirmed as everyone else in the belief that I place love of the equine before anything in human shape.'

With a sardonic bow he strode away from Destine, and she was left to ponder his cynical words as she made her way back to the patio where Cosima was now in close conversation with an elderly member of the Castros household, a rather forbidding dowager, indulged by the household, and with a crisply ironed *mantilla* covering her white hair. In her hand was a large fan, ivory-handled, and on a table at her elbow a glass of sherry and a plate of small iced biscuits.

Destine hesitated, but Cosima caught sight of her and beckoned her to join them. 'Señora Castros, this is my English nurse who, I might tell you, has bullied me out of my bedroom into the warm sunlight. Oh, I agree, she is only slight, but she has a very determined character.'

The dowager swept her shrewd eyes over Destine and in that way that was so Latin she seemed to make her feel very young, much less the cool and collected nurse who had been looking after people for close on ten years. The ivory-handled fan opened in the gnarled hand and there were red roses embroidered on the lace, perhaps a relic of the dowager's days of youth and flirtation.

'You must join us in a sherry, miss, and you must talk about London and that remarkable shop called Harrods, and tell me if they still serve tea and cucumber sandwiches in the lounge of the Ritz after one has been shopping at Harrods.'

Like most educated Latins the dowager had a remarkable command of English, with that sibilant emphasis on certain words that made them seem – more exciting, somehow. Destine broke into a smile as she sat down in the cane chair which Cosima indicated.

'I'm afraid, *señora*, that our English nursing service doesn't pay enough for its nurses to shop at Harrods, or take tea at the Ritz. But I'm sure both establishments are still as glamorous as they always were.'

145

'But if you are the clever nurse that Cosima tells me you are, then why are you not paid enough? I thought your country was far more advanced in these things than we are in Spain. Of a far greater sophistication when it comes to its working classes. You are of that class, are you not?'

'Yes, *señora*.' Destine didn't lose her composure, for she knew that a streak of dominant snobbishness ran in the veins of Latin women of the upper classes. From childhood they had servants to wait on them, and anyone who worked for a living had, for them, the status of a servant. All the same Destine couldn't help comparing this woman to the Marquesa de Obregon who had a grace of breeding that held no hint of condescension towards her daughter's nurse. Life had been kinder to this dowager who lived among her sons and their children, but it was the Marquesa who had the tenderness and the kind of beauty that was unimpaired by the acid of a sharp tongue. Even Cosima would never have the graciousness of her mother, but just recently Destine had begun to wonder if the Don had some of his aunt's gallantry tucked away in a secret corner of his heart.

A manservant had obeyed the signal of the lace fan and a glass of sherry had been placed on the table for Destine. '*Salud*,' she murmured, as she picked up the fluted glass and took a sip of the rich golden wine that probably came from the cellars of the *finca*. Each of these families – or rightly these dynasties – had their own vines, from which their own brand of sherry was distilled and bottled.

It seemed a pride, almost a way of life for each establishment to try and outdo the others in the matter of superior sherry, more virile sons, finer horses, and lovelier women. It was a feudal system, and Destine felt many miles removed from the modern life of London, as if time had turned backwards and she found herself in the nineteenth century, a girl whose dress seemed to expose too much leg for the scrutiny of the Señora Castros.

146

She glanced away and it was quite by chance that she happened to look in the direction of the table where several male members of the party were taking wine and more robust snacks than iced biscuits. 'What do you think of Spain and its men?' The question came sharply, curiously. Destine felt a youthful compulsion to pull at the hem of her simple dress, which instead of making her inconspicuous now seemed to underline her difference from the raven-haired, golden-skinned young women of the south.

'Do you find our men good-looking?' the *señora* insisted. 'I see that my sons and their friends compel your blue eyes—blue always seems to me such a deceptively innocent colour, but I understand that Nordic women discard their innocence as soon as possible.'

Destine glanced back at the dowager, and caught the amused look that Cosima cast at her, as if to challenge her to try and get the better of the Spanish woman steeped in having her own way, and probably never opposed by the wives of her sons and the *novias* of her nephews.

'I imagine that in all countries there will always be girls who can be tempted by persuasive men. I don't imagine, *señora*, that the iron grille at Spanish windows is always effective in keeping Don Juan at bay, for I have a godmother in Madrid who is the benefactress of a home where young women of your country go to have their babies. It really isn't fair to brand Nordic women as shameless, and to pretend that all Latin girls are speckless. The truth is that all human beings are frail or strong in the face of—love.'

Having stated her case Destine took a deep sip of her sherry. She wasn't a Latin girl and she wasn't going to be browbeaten by the matriarch of the Castros family. It was enraging that because she was English she was supposed to swoon at the sight of a Spaniard.

'Are you in love, miss, to speak so emphatically on the emotion?' The *señora* reached out and patted Destine on the

147

left wrist with her fan, which she had closed with a snap. 'Will you be frail, or strong, when this man persuades you to open your window one night, when the *dama de noche* opens in the courtyard and turns your head with its perfume?'

'The man I love was killed,' Destine said simply. 'I came to Spain to work, not to – to have my head turned by a handsome Spaniard and the flower of the night. Thank goodness I'm not a foolish girl any more.'

'It would be foolishness to suppose that the girl ever leaves the soul of a woman.' The old *señora* stared hard at Destine for a moment, and then a thin smile edged her lips. 'The body ages, miss, but the feminine heart ever quickens that some man might still say, "*A sus pies, guapa!*"'

'Really, I want no man at my feet,' Destine replied. 'In fact it must be one of those exaggerated Latin claims, for I just can't imagine any Spaniard in that humble position. He strikes me as being far too proud and confident to ever make a doormat of himself.'

'You'd be contemptuous of the doormat, eh, and would want a man to be your master?' The dowager spread her fan and took a deliberate look around the large patio. 'She wants him *muy hombre*, but my sons are married men, and my nephews are bespoken, and half the region knows that Don Cicatrice has waited years to marry you, Cosima. You are out of luck, miss, if you want one of our Spaniards. They are the property of Spanish girls.'

'Who are welcome to them,' Destine said, her coolness vanishing in a wave of heat. 'I didn't come to the *finca* to find a man but to keep an eye on my patient. Your sons, *señora*, your nephews, and anyone else's *novio* are quite safe from my designs – good heavens, are all English women treated in Spain as if they have nothing to do but seduce the men? I, for one, find Spaniards too much a mixture of pepper and steel to want a closer relationship, and I'm quite

148

happy to be left among the images, as I believe the term is for a woman *soledad*.'

'Such temper in a seemingly self-contained young woman,' mocked the old woman, fluttering her fan and with a gleam in her eyes. 'Look how the paleness has vanished and given way to wild roses – and so you call yourself *soledad*, eh? You think you can live alone, with no man to wrap his arms around you when the nights are cold and the siesta a little too warm? You think it will be easy, eh, never to have a child rush from its play into your arms? You must have lots of courage, miss, for to be the lonely virgin is not the kind of fate that any Spanish girl would wish upon herself.'

'I hope I have courage,' Destine said, with dignity. 'At least I know what it is to have been married to a good, kind man.'

'Cosima tells me he was killed on your wedding day?'

'Yes – ' Destine caught at her bottom lip and some of the old bitterness swept over her and she wanted to blurt out that a Spaniard had been responsible for Matt's death and the last thing on earth she wanted was to replace him in her heart with a man of Latin blood.

'Better to lose a man that way than any other.' The sharp eyes darted to Cosima and then back to Destine, and it came as an inexpressible relief when a long shadow fell across the table and the voice of Don Cicatrice broke in on the conversation.

'Are you catching up on all the old scandals and hearing of the new ones, Cosima *mia*?' he asked, and the strong smoke of a *cigarro* drifted downwards and wafted into Destine's face, almost with the shock of a blow. It was a blend of tobacco entirely personal to him, and the smoke seemed to penetrate into her pores as he stood making casual conversation with the two Latin women, a tinge of sardonic humour in the deep timbre of his voice.

Destine sat there with her fingers locked about the stem of

149

her sherry glass, for even as the mother of the Castros brothers made answer to his remarks, she darted several inquisitive looks across the table, to where Destine sat in the shadow of the Don. Her heart thumped. What did the woman think . . . that because she dwelt at the Casera de los Rejas, and because she was young and not exactly hideous, she was of some sort of interest to the Don?

I can't bear this for very much longer, she thought. Being an object of curiosity to these people who find it so impossible for any woman, young or old, to be disinterested in men!

'Well, *hombre,* what did you think of Saladin?' Fernando Castros had approached and as he spoke he slapped the Don on the shoulder. The taller man turned and the sun struck with sudden brazen cruelty across his scarred face. Even as Destine looked at the two men, so did Cosima, and she seemed to stare at the good-looking Fernando with a sudden bleakness in her eyes.

She's thinking of Miguel! The words flashed through Destine's mind. She's remembering how appealing he is, with something of the appearance and the charm of Fernando Castros. She's wondering how she can live without Miguel, but that won't stop her from marrying the Don. She has to prove to these people that she can marry again, and it won't matter to her—afterwards—if she makes life a hell for that tall man standing there with irony in his eyes.

'It's one devil of a good-looking animal,' the Don drawled, in answer to Fernando's query. 'But can it run—really run, my friend, so that it beats my Primitivo?'

'Are you making a challenge, *amigo?*' Fernando drew himself up very straight, but still he remained a head shorter than the other man.

The Don lifted his *cigarro* with a lazy movement of his hand, and yet his entire body seemed charged with a force never fully dispelled, not even after a long day in the plantations. He wouldn't be afraid of any challenge, for it wouldn't really matter to him if he won or lost. It was the actual physical effort that he enjoyed; the feel of a fine horse going at full gallop across the *sabana*, the rush of the wind in his face, the cares of the mind lost for a while in the pleasure of the ride.

'What will you bet?' Fernando asked him. 'There is more fun if there is a prize to be won.'

'Is there?' the Don cast an enigmatic smile across the patio. 'What have I, *amigo*, that you prize?'

'The horse Primitivo itself,' said the other Spaniard, and there was a sudden sharp look in his eyes that reminded Destine of his mother. 'Do you still dare to ride if my Arab outdistances your mount? I know you set great store by your animal, but do you dare to gamble with him?'

The Don considered this, gazing at the smouldering tip of his dark *cigarro*. 'No,' he said at last. 'I know that Primitivo can outride your horse, Fernando, but I ride only for pleasure. My regrets, *amigo*, but I don't chase the hare, only the wind.'

'You are backing out?' Fernando exclaimed.

'One can't back out of something one hasn't entered.' The *cigarro* was dropped into an ashtray and ground to a black stub with a decisive movement of the lean dark hand. Destine watched with a kind of fascination and listened intently. Always in Latin conversation there seemed layers of meaning ... an arabesque of words twining around a central theme, and right now it seemed to her that Fernando Castros was trying to prove himself the superior man, more daring than the Don, more willing to gamble with his goods.

'I've never known you to be chicken-hearted before,' he gibed. 'If I lost the race to you, then you would have Saladin. Do you hear me weeping because I might lose something for which I paid a lot of money?'

'What of that?' Don Cicatrice shrugged his shoulders.

151

'Primitivo was a wild, free colt whom I roped in the hills. I paid no more for him than a few bruises and some oats. His value lies in the pleasure he and I have found together when we ride. I don't just own him, Fernando. He means more to me than that, and I wouldn't cheapen what I value by placing it on the table of chance.'

A short silence followed his words, and then Fernando gave a laugh. 'I remember Manolito once saying that you never once saw him fight in a *corrida*. I wonder, *amigo*, if that fire long ago took the fire out of you?'

Even as Destine heard what Fernando said, she leapt to her feet and before she could control herself she had flung the remainder of her sherry into the taunting, good-looking face. There were gasps of shock from his mother and from the other women who witnessed the way she hurled the wine so that it ran down the olive-skinned face and spattered the white shirt front.

She didn't care a jot. It had been the note of admiration in his voice when he mentioned Manolito as much as the cruelty of his remark which had propelled her to her feet, driven to the edge of control and beyond it by the Don's stony acceptance of the insult.

'How would you like to be burned?' she asked angrily as Fernando pulled out a handkerchief and mopped his wet face. 'I've seen people and children brought into hospital with burns, and there's nothing on earth more awful than their suffering. You—arrogant and sure of yourself, and surrounded by your family, what do you know about suffering? You should be ashamed of yourself for saying such a thing!'

'What is happening—what is wrong?' Susana had come running from the house, followed by a small girl who began to cry.

'Hush! It is nothing! Of no moment at all!' In a couple of strides Don Cicatrice had reached the child and bending down he swung her to his shoulder. 'Ah, how much bigger you have grown, Perdida, since last I saw you. Come, there is no need for tears. Your papa, I assure you, is not crying— he has a little wine in his eye, that is all.'

And distinctly, even in the midst of her distress, Destine caught the note of sardonic humour in his voice.

Susana stared at her husband, reaching out a hand to feel the dampness of his shirt. His mother had risen to her feet and the look she directed at Destine was one of fearful dignity. 'How dare you do such a thing to my son?' she boomed out.

'I—I'm sure he'll recover,' Destine said, and she could now feel herself shaking with reaction. 'A little sherry in the face certainly won't leave him with a scar.'

'You—you impertinent snip!' The dowager raised her fan, and at once Susana caught at her mother-in-law's arm and held it in abeyance. Her pretty face was distressed as she looked at Destine, and then at her husband, who still seemed unable to believe that any woman would throw the dregs of her wine in his handsome face.

'Won't someone please explain—'

It was Cosima who broke the tension by bursting into a peal of laughter. 'Fernando, you look so *hurt*. And my dear Destine, you really don't need to leap to the defence of my *novio*. He's quite used to people making remarks about his face, and he's really quite hardened. Heaven help me, what a comedy. It's quite made my day!'

'It's ruined my shirt,' Fernando snapped, and then to Destine's sheer amazement she learned why Spaniards had a reputation for being unexpected.

'You have a good aim, *señorita*.' He gave her a quizzical smile and seemed to forget that she was not a single girl. 'You also have a quick temper, so heaven help the man who marries you, and let us hope he stocks up well on shirts before the wedding day.'

'Come, *querido*, let us go and find you another shirt.'

153

Susana took her husband by the arm and led him towards the house. On their way they passed Don Cicatrice with their small daughter, and through the rain of the fountain Destine watched, numbly, as Fernando paused and said something very quietly to the Don. He inclined his dark head, and Destine noticed that the chattering Perdida was totally unafraid of the lean scarred face.

CHAPTER SEVEN

THAT day at the *finca* was rounded off by a *musica y danza,*
which went on after a general siesta, when the guests followed the example of the family and rested in cool rooms
beneath purring fans until the afternoon sun began to lose
some of its intense heat.

Destine shared a small side room with a young cousin of
the hostess, and as she lay on a divan in the shade of the
drawn louvres she tried to close her mind to memory . . .
she ached to fall asleep as easily as the Spanish girl, but as
the minutes ticked by she lay relentlessly awake and at the
mercy of the images that kept racing across her mind.

She pressed her hot face into the cushion of her couch . . .
she didn't really care that she had made Fernando Castros
look undignified in front of his wife and friends; what concerned her and made her feel so restive was that her action
with the sherry had been so instinctive that nothing on earth
would have stopped her from reacting like . . . like some
vixen defending its cub.

As a nurse she could tell from the Don's scarring that he
had suffered acutely at the time of the accident, and as she
had stormed at Fernando Castros there was hardly another
pain that was so unbearable, so racking, so close to hell on
earth as a third-degree burn. The actual recovery from shock
and pain was torment in itself, and she would have flung an
entire bucket of water in that self-complacent, unspoiled face
if one had been handy.

She hated cruelty . . . yes, that was why she had reacted so
fiercely. There had been nothing personal in it, and yet it
must have looked so much like the action of a woman
personally concerned . . . perhaps involved with Don Cica-

155

trice, the bespoken of Cosima Arandas, who could never leap to her feet in defence of the man she was supposed to love.

Love . . . oh no, Destine turned restively and wished with every atom of her body that she could slip away from the *finca* and not have to face those curious, and accusing eyes when siesta was over and the party reassembled for the evening. What excuse could she make to go when it would only look as if she were running away? No, she had to stay and face the music . . . that of guitars and castanets.

It wasn't the first *musica y danza* she had attended in Spain, but it was quite unlike those parties arranged by her godmother in the more sophisticated city of Madrid, where evening dress was worn and the food was served daintily on china plates, while a smooth trio of guitar players strummed the well-known melodies of the Latin world.

Here at the *finca* a whole pig was roasted on an outdoor spit, and on a long wooden table set beneath the trees of the patio, on big plates of polished copper, were piles of devil-led corn garnished with tomatoes and peppers, bowls of shrimp and avocado salad, trellised pastries stuffed with meat and onion, spiced sausages, baby marrows, roast potatoes, and an enormous apple and cherry pie coated with rich brown sugar. The entire feast looked good and smelled delicious, and on a smaller table stood straw-wrapped jars of strong Spanish wine, alongside bottles of sherry, manzanilla, and brandy. For the younger people and the children there were pitchers of fruit juice and a punch made from sliced peaches and passion-fruit.

The party, announced Susana, had been arranged directly Cosima had given her word that she would come for the day. But now that Cosima planned at some future date to become the wife of Don Cicatrice, then there was added reason for a celebration.

Fernando, looking very much himself again in a sleek

dark suit and a frilled shirt, encircled his wife's waist with his arm, and it seemed to Destine that his eyes skimmed her face a moment before he looked directly at Cosima and the Don. 'All of us here,' he said clearly, 'wish our two friends the best of future happiness. I have known Artez since we were boys, and we even did our military service together. I don't hold it against him that he has an iron seat and can ride any horse, even those of the Spanish cavalry at Cuerto, where we often galloped in the desert, and I know that he won't use an iron hand to keep his wife as good, sweet and obedient as mine. It is good, right, that a Spaniard should marry a girl of his own people, for the Spanish girl is like the carnation, she has no thorns to stab a man.'

Applause greeted Fernando's speech, and as Destine stood tense near a lovely weeping fuchsia, a tall figure came to her side and quietly slid a glass into her hand. She glanced at Lugh Davidson in the golden light of the wall-lanterns and saw that he was looking at her with gravely enquiring eyes.

'Aren't you afraid that I shall go crazy again with a glass of sherry?' she asked him, a little twist to her lips.

'It was a trifle unexpected.' His dark brows contracted. 'One somehow expects a fiery Latin to react in that way, but you look so – so cool and composed.'

'It just goes to show, Lugh, that you can't judge a book from its jacket.' She lifted her sherry and tasted it a trifle defiantly. 'Are you, like everyone else, judging me now as the secret *amarata* of the Don who couldn't endure to have him mocked for his scarred face? The truth,' she gave a cynical little laugh, 'is far less romantic. He and I couldn't be more opposed to each other. We're ice and flame – oil and water – hare and hound. It's just that as a nurse I've seen badly burned people admitted into hospital, and any nurse or doctor will tell you that of all the injuries they have to deal with a case of burning or scalding really shakes them.

157

Burn cases don't scream, they quietly moan with an agony that is beyond screaming. Had I been Susana, who looks as if she has been fed on cream and kisses all her life, I daresay her husband's remark would have slid off my mind like a drop of oil. But I know a little about suffering and I reacted – instinctively. That's all I know – there's nothing personal between Don Cicatrice and myself. He doesn't altogether like me. He has shown that on more than one occasion, and though I can't assure these other people that I'm not his light of love, I wanted you to know.'

After that it was a little easier for Destine to enjoy the evening festivities and the food, wandering with Lugh, plate in hand, and talking to him with an ease that had been absent from their encounter earlier that day. Maybe because she had revealed that she wasn't as cool and controlled as she looked, but was still very much a girl at the mercy of her feelings.

She felt a sort of protectiveness in the Welshman, as if she had found a friend in place of the suitor she hadn't wanted. The moon rose over the *finca* and seemed to swing in the purple sky like a big golden bell. From beneath the shrubs stole the scented breath of heaven, and pale showers of vine-rose glimmered beneath the filigreed patio lamps. The night, the people and the music had a strange beauty, and Destine believed that nothing would be more evocative of the Spain she would remember than the *sal española* of the dancing couple who sprang to the centre of the patio and faced each other like a pair of beautiful tigers. The girl wore a polka-dot dress of red and white, profusely frilled, and the man, with black sideburns running down to his chiselled chin, had on a skin-tight black suit, the frills of his shirt-front gleaming white as his teeth.

Destine caught her breath at the sheer physical beauty of the couple, as still as if caught on the canvas of a Goya a moment before the polished castanets began to click on the

girl's upraised hands, her fingers pushed through the coloured bands of the shell-shaped instruments that were like the
heartbeat of this land.

The couple began to dance, the man so dark and sensuous
against the twirling skirts of the girl. They were the *los
amantes* of Spanish legend, the desert blood still running
strongly in their veins under the golden skin. They touched,
then withdrew; they were caressing and then they were
cruel, taunting each other with their pliant bodies and their
lashing eyes.

It was a ravishing scene set against the thick white walls of
the *finca* and the shade of Moorish alcoves, in which seemed
trapped the scent of spice and dark leaves. Destine was
unaware that she had moved away from Lugh, whose eyes
were pinned upon the dancing girl, until she found herself
alone in one of the alcoves, pressed back against the wall as
if she wanted to hide herself, and she was almost hidden by a
cascading plume of purple bougainvillaea.

Something wet and warm rolled slowly down her cheek
and she wiped away a tear with no real sense of surprise.
That was why she had drawn away from Lugh, because of
this sudden ache in her heart ... this awareness that tonight
marked for her the beginning of her farewell to Spain. She
had fought not to feel this way about Manolito's country ...
she had wanted only the bitterness, never the poignancy of
a Spanish night drenched in flower and moonlight and the
throb of music from the Moorish courts of love.

Love ... she caught her breath. Why did she have to
think of love when it had nothing to do with her; when the
music and the magic of the night were for those who had
someone to whom they could turn in a security deeper and
stronger than the fleeting passion of the senses?

She sighed and heard the rustling of bougainvillaea petals
... a tall figure emerged and, dark and shadowed, she took
him for Lugh, come in search of her. 'So there you are!' The

man spoke, and the deep voice went through Destine like a knife, for it wasn't the voice of the Welshman but that of the man whom she had imagined with the woman he was bound to marry.

He came closer and a shaft of moonlight struck him and made his dark head seem darker, and she saw the play of shadows around his lips and the lean strength of his jaw. She had not spoken to him since that incident of the sherry, and now there swept over her such an awful feeling of shyness that she couldn't answer him but could only stand there with desperation in her eyes. Why couldn't he have left her alone? Was he curious, like the others? Did he want to know why she had defended him? Well, there wasn't any answer that made sense when he was so big and powerful and so obviously capable of fighting his own battles.

'What do you want?' Suddenly her jaw unlocked and she was able to speak, only to sound as if she resented him for intruding upon her.

'I lost sight of you—I suppose I wanted to find out if you were enjoying the music and the dancing. Are you?' His voice was quite impersonal, but that thin lance of moonlight that stabbed through the bougainvillaea and across his face revealed the twitch of a muscle beside his mouth, and Destine had the sudden feeling that there was something tensely controlled about him, that a look, a word, even a slight movement from her would release him from that lethal control. Her breath quickened and her hands were pressing into the wall behind her, almost bruisingly. The magic of the night, the enchantment, had drawn closer . . . but in a frightening way.

'They're exciting,' she said, and she had to strive to keep her voice steady. 'The real and the forbidden that someone like me is fortunate to have seen and heard. The tourist in Madrid or Seville is really missing something.'

'That's true.' A curt edge to his voice seemed to touch the

160

nerves just under Destine's skin. He swung a hand and petals fell, stroking against her skin so that she shivered. 'It isn't everyone who comes to Spain who is allowed to catch a glimpse of our true way of life. We remain, especially so in the south, a feudal people who cling to the old traditions because they have a fervour and an integrity that is more satisfying than the modern way of life.'

The music beyond the curtain of flowers, so dense over the arcade that anyone glancing this way wouldn't see that it was occupied, had changed to the *marimba,* a dulcet sound that mingled romantically with the feminine laughter and the drifting scent of woodsmoke.

'No stranger,' he said, 'could ever really understand our ways. You were angered by Fernando for no real reason, for we accept pain as we accept pleasure; we enjoy the triumphs and the tragedies of life in equal measure. Fatalism is the marrow of our bones, and it has a strange way of making most things endurable.'

'It seems a cruel philosophy to me,' she said. 'It means that if you can accept pain almost with pride, then you can inflict it. I imagine that's how the Spanish Inquisition came into being, and how a Golden Age for Spain was made possible by slavery.'

'England had her share of slaves,' he said ironically. 'Children of ten were working down her coal pits, and men died by the score on her tropic plantations, literally worked to death for the white gold known as sugar. In every human being there is a seed of cruelty, *señora.* Only the angels are perfect, and would I sound too much a devil if I said that the angelic can be a trifle tedious?'

'I could never imagine you consorting with angels, *señor.*' Her tension found a little relief as she smiled at his remark. 'Half angels, perhaps, for you're not altogether a devil—'

There she broke off, confused, alarmed, like someone who had dashed headlong into a patch of brambles. And there

161

was no way to extricate herself, for he had heard her quite distinctly and she could feel him looking down at her even as she turned her eyes swiftly from his face.

'That is quite a confession from a girl who avowed that I was devilish.' He spoke drily, and yet with a lazy deepening of his voice that sent a wave of emotion over Destine. When he spoke like that there was a sensuous, almost caressing quality to his words, making her aware of the brown throat from which they arose, a column of warmth and strength, pulsing with the vital life force of the man. Her fingers dug into the stone of the arcade as if to benumb the incredible urge to feel the warm neck of the Don between her hands.

What in heaven's name had got into her ... all day she had been like someone possessed of an alien force!

'I must go – ' the words scraped her throat. 'Lugh will be wondering what has become of me – '

'So already you call him by his first name, eh?'

'It's quite usual, in my country,' she rejoined. 'The use of first names is quite a casual thing.'

'So I was incorrect in thinking that you didn't want the intimate attentions of this man?'

'Don't be absurd – ' She caught her breath. 'Intimacy has nothing to do with it. He's friendly and we speak the same language, and it's just like a Latin to read headlines where there is really only small print!'

'Perhaps that is because we are so intrigued by the inscrutable mysteries of life – and love.'

'Love!' she exclaimed. 'Do you imagine I've fallen in love like some convent girl let out among men for the first time?'

'In some ways you have been in a kind of seclusion – a self-imposed chastity to do with being a bride and widow on the very same day.'

'That, señor, doesn't mean that I am now ready to break whatever vows I took to myself when Matthew died. I'm not a Spanish girl! I could never give myself to a man I didn't

162

love with every fraction of my heart, every nerve of my body, and every cell of my soul!'

'You say that with great conviction, but have you considered loneliness?'

'A nurse is never lonely, *señor*.'

'I talk about her when she is off duty and closes the door on her patients and those who work alongside her. Then there can be only the ticking of the clock, or the infernally cheerful voice of the radio announcer, never giving her the satisfaction of a flash of temper, and offering only the jest that a million other women will share. Rather than endure that, it is very much easier for a Spanish girl to give herself to a man who will be tolerably good to her. Spaniards don't make ideal husbands, but they are rarely boring.'

'It all sounds very cold-blooded to me.' Destine, on the other hand, didn't feel a sense of coldness, only a quickening of alarm as the Don stretched an arm to the wall and casually enclosed her in an angle of the arcade. Then he seemed taller than ever, indescribably closer, so that she breathed the tang of his own special tobacco on his clothing, and the more subtle aroma of his warm skin. The racing pulse in her throat felt as if it might choke her, and as panic spread through her body she wanted to thrust herself out of his way before ... oh God, before what? He touched her and it became impossible to ever pretend again that he meant nothing to her.

'Cold blood can never flow between a man and a woman, and what you really mean to say is that it seems unromantic that a Spaniard should be shrewd about marriage rather than reckless.' He gave a laugh so brief it was almost a growl. 'The English are so amusing. They insist on being as cool as a cucumber in the face of cannon and curse, and the truth is that the worm of reality eats away at their romantic hearts, even as their women flirt on the beaches with young men who will marry the girl chosen for them by their grandmother, and the men sit in the cafés and stare at the flamenco dancers who at home have two or three *pequeñas*. The Latin is a realist, *señora*. He only looks as if he might be Rudolph Valentino.'

'What is he in reality, *señor*?' Destine just couldn't resist asking, and curiously enough she felt no real resentment at the way he mocked the English. He was so incredibly right about them. At the deep heart of them they were the romantic gallants of the world, sons and daughters of a selfless, sacrificial past, a people who could still be rallied to fiercely defend their green and crazy island. Images rushed through the brain when anyone thought of England, barbaric under Roman rule, but ready with pike and incredible loyalty by the time the Vikings were rowing their longboats along the bird-haunted marshes, steely eyes glittering through their helmets and terrible enough to make any heart quake but that of the villagers, the monks, the knights who rushed to the side of their king and conquered one of the strongest, cruellest, most pagan of foes. And there were the chalk cliffs tumbled to the sea were the blood-red poppies on their delicate stems ... symbols of all the dying, all the loving given to a land that was still the most glorious of all.

Destine lifted her chin and her blue eyes shone with a quiet pride. 'I know the English, *señor*. I knew my husband, but tell me, what is a Spaniard?'

A silence prevailed as he considered her question, and she stood there, tensely more aware of this man of another nation, of a totally different ideology from her own, than she had ever been of anyone ... even the man she had married. Her heart felt shaken, and her body felt curiously defenceless as she pressed herself against the wall, as far away from him as possible.

'Strange as it may seem, *señora*, the typical Spaniard does not resemble Don Juan and is much more in the mould of Don Quixote. His respect for honour is almost religious in its intensity and he wouldn't think twice about defending his honour by cutting to the bone the throat of his detractor. I feel you shudder, but you asked for the truth, did you not?'

'Yes,' she whispered, and beyond the wide spread of his shoulders and the soft rustling of petals she could hear the pulsing rhythm of the Latin music . . . passion, symbolism, threat.

'The flamenco dance is a duel between a man and a woman,' he said. 'It is sensual and yet it imposes a restraint that makes even the brush of her frilled skirts against his person a beautiful and forbidden caress. Watch the dance carefully and not once will you see the couple actually touch each other, not in public, not in front of the crowd, who are yet made unbearably aware that they watch a dance of passion. It is in the nature of the Spaniard to hate a display of his innermost feelings and in front of other people he may often show indifference or downright coldness to the person most closely attached to him. It is, of course, a different matter within the high walls of his home, behind the iron grilles of his windows. He may even be ruled by the woman in private, but his public image must always be that of a proud man. Sensuality may repose in his lips, his glance and sometimes in what he says, but he kisses only in private, except for the courtesy kiss on the wrist of an elderly relative. In lots of ways he is cloaked in his reserve, but at heart he carries the lance of Quixote and he tilts at strange dreams—the *saudade* in his soul; the search for the impossible.'

'And you call that being unromantic?' A smile came, fled around Destine's lips, and then was gone as with a shocking suddenness the Don dropped his hand to her shoulder and she seemed to feel his touch right through her skin to her bones, so that a tingling, electric dart sped to the very core of her.

'Don't!' The word broke from her like a gasp of pain.

'I shan't, when you have answered a question of mine. Why defend this cicatrice of mine when you flinch from it? Why make a drama of a farce, eh?'

'Farce?' The word choked her. 'Do you have to be so cynical?'

'Perhaps cynicism saves me from sinfulness. There are times when it would be an inexpressible relief to sin – even you – even you must have felt this, *mi bruja blanca*.'

My white witch!

Destine held her breath, and then lost it, almost completely, as with an abrupt savagery she was swept close to the Don, his hands biting into her body. '*El momento de la verdad*, that is how it is in the arena when the raised sword glitters in the sun. A moment of terrible truth! Tell me now that you hate me – tell me!'

She tried, desperately, but his arms were around her and she could feel their strength and their warmth right through the material of her dress, holding her so forcibly that her dress was drawn up from the warm crevices at the back of her shaking knees. This wasn't the first time she had been in his arms, but never before had there been this instant and overwhelming desire to stay in them, locked close in her slimness to the power and strength of his body.

Hate ... the lost memory of hating him spun out of the orbit of her mind and her body and all she was aware of was a warm languor as her head tilted back against his arm and her lips received his without struggle or surprise, or the will to ever break away from the ravishing sensation that she felt as his hard mouth seemed to melt into her own and she was pressed with a punishing tenderness to his heart.

When, groaning, he drew his lips away and buried them in the soft side of her neck, she gave way at last to what wouldn't be denied and clasping his head with her hands she pressed her lips to his scar, running them up and down the cicatrice, as if in this way to ease the memory of his pain.

166

'We kiss like this, but it can never happen again.' He spoke the words against her skin, so that the very movement of his lips seemed like a caress before the torture. 'You must leave Xanas very soon; you will return to your own country and you will – forget me.'

'And will you do the same, Artez – forget?' Her voice was choked with the anguish of the held-in tears. Her fingers dug into him and no longer was he the dark and distant stranger who used mockery to shield this heart that felt as if it wanted to join itself to hers, beating hard against her, only the silk of his shirt a second skin between them. The image of him there in the perfumed darkness made her feel dizzy, his black hair across his brow and his mouth a brand of desire across the quivering, silent cries in her throat.

Oh, God ... he seemed a part of her as no one else had ever been ... not even Matthew.

No, not even Matt, so kind, so clever and courtly. Never had she flared into anger with him; never had there been this tumult of mixed pleasure and pain.

'Ah, Don Cicatrice,' she whispered, unable to raise her voice for the weight of his mouth. 'I think I'll die if I have to go away from you.'

'Dying isn't that easy, *ninita*. Sinning is a lot easier and it will come to that if you stay where I can see you each day and be aware of you each night. I am not a free and youthful Spaniard who can play *dragonear* at your window. *Por cierto*, I must climb in through that window, or I must send you away. You understand me. I don't have to be explicit, do I?'

She shook her head against him, and was more aware than ever of the hard strength to which surrender would be heaven ... and hell afterwards when she had to see him with Cosima. He would never hurt Cosima. What he felt for her had nothing to do with this hard physical need which Destine felt in him. He was strong enough to control desire,

167

but he had no defence against the compassion which Cosima aroused. He would marry her . . . and send Destine away from him.

'It has to be,' he said. '*Ay,* if only you had gone that first day, then it would have been a clean cut without the torn flesh. This cicatrice on my face will be nothing to the one inside me. *Mierda!* Why did you have to come to Xanas with your hair like a silver flame and your eyes blue as the heaven we can never share? Why couldn't your hate be real—I sometimes believed that it might be, until you flung sherry into the handsome face of Fernando. *Por dios,* it took all my control not to sweep you into my arms when you did that. I wanted to hold you, and then take you far away with me. No woman should be so—so beautiful!'

'Ah—' the little cry was torn from her as he suddenly thrust her away from him and turned with animal instinct away from her, brushing through the curtain of bougain-villaea.

'I am coming, Sanchez,' she heard him say. 'I was being solitary and indulging in a day-dream, *amigo.*'

'Cosima wants you,' said the other man. 'I believe she is feeling fatigued and would like to be taken home.'

'I am at her service,' said Don Cicatrice as they went out of earshot. Destine trembled, for she hadn't caught the approach of Sanchez as the Don had. Another moment and he would have caught them together and there would have been no way to avoid scandal, for the Don's arms had been holding her.

She still felt as if they were hard and warm around her, but the truth was that she was alone as never before, the 'other woman' in the life of a Spaniard who was honour bound to put duty before desire.

Desire . . . was it only a physical flame that burned be-tween them, that time and distance would extinguish? 'You must go away,' he had said. 'You must—forget me.'

Forget the way she had reacted to his kisses ... to the closeness of his strength and his control. She had sensed that control and it had been far more exciting than if, like other men, he had allowed his body to be his master. It proved his power and his superiority, and it gave some indication of the superb lover he would be.

Destine pressed her hands to her burning face. It was incredible that she should feel this way about a man to whom she could never belong in an honourable way. It was a realisation from which she wanted to flee ... something to which she wanted to run with arms outflung and her heart thrown open, uncaring of his people and their southern code of honour.

A terrible code that bound him to a woman who would never give him her love, or a son of his splendid body.

A choked sob broke from Destine. She who wanted to cry out her love had, instead, to hide it as if it were something shameful. She had to behave as if the Don meant no more to her than the aloof nephew of her employer. Aloof ... could she ever pretend again that he was distant and arrogant when she had been close enough to have felt the turbulent beating of his heart? Could she look at him with cool eyes when her veins seemed to run molten each time she remembered his lips against her skin?

Could she leave him when she wanted so much to love him? Yes, she loved Don Cicatrice – not in the way she had cared for Matt, but in a way so different that there was no sense of betrayal. Her kind and generous Matthew would not begrudge the reawakening of her heart, and her senses ... senses she had not been aware of until the Don had aroused them under the savagely tender assault of his lips.

And on that awakening she must turn her back, going her lonely way, leaving behind her that tall, scarred personage who would marry to become a protector rather than a lover.

169

The prospect was chilling and all the warmth had seeped out of Destine's body and she felt cold . . . abandoned. Even as she found love again, she had to let go of it. Neither she nor the Don were natural sinners, so from now on, in the words of Rupert Brooke, it must be:

'*Each in his lonely night, each with a ghost.*'

The farewells were affectionate. 'You must come again, both of you!' Susana Castros hugged Cosima, and dared to do the same to Don Cicatrice. Then she looked at Destine with cooler eyes. 'You will be going home to England, eh? Now that our precious Cosima is restored to health?'

'Yes.' Destine's decision was as final as that, and she was glad to get into the car beside Cosima, and to share the lap-robe that the Don flung over both sets of knees. The top of the car had been closed down, and the interior began to warm up as soon as they were on the road, speeding away from the lights of the *finca* and the waving hands.

'*Hasta la vista,*' Cosima murmured, her head tiredly at rest against the glowing leather of the back seat. 'It was good to see them all, but now I feel weary. I think I shall sleep. *Dios,* how Artez keeps his vitality so intact I shall never know.' She yawned delicately and her head drooped sideways, resting on Destine's shoulder. She felt light even in sleep, fragile and wistful as a child being taken home from a party. And like a child how could she be hurt by those whom she trusted? The man she loved had let her down, but the man she didn't love would never do so.

Destine's eyes dwelt on his dark head and his broad shoulders, and she wanted to reach out and touch him, and felt in the silence a strong sense of communication with him. He had heard what she had replied to Susana Castros . . . even as it had begun between them, it had ended.

They arrived at the *casa,* and Cosima was still drowsy and half asleep as the Don carried her to her apartment. Destine

170

said she would assist the *señora* into her bed, but he firmly shook his head and pressed the bell that brought Anaya to the bedroom. 'You are weary yourself,' he said to Destine, and with a hand clasping her wrist he led her across the hall to the staircase. 'The emotions are in a turmoil, eh?' he murmured.

She nodded, and her heart gave a throb as she looked at him and saw the slumbrous fire in his eyes. She gave him a smile, strained out of the secret torment and pleasure of knowing he wanted her. She swayed a little towards him, knowing she was clay when she must be adamant – but, oh, to sin with him would be greater than having to cling to chastity when she loved him from his flame-seared face to the very soles of his silent feet.

He stared down at her pale face and his own face had a curiously drawn look beneath the bronzed skin. 'Go away soon,' he said harshly. 'Go before I hurt you, and Cosima.'

'You could never hurt me,' she said in a low, tense voice. 'I think if you raised your hand and struck me to the ground I'd still go on – caring.'

'Caring?' He took a harsh breath and began to lead her up the stairs to the gallery where the lamps half-glimmered and everything had that dreamlike quality that the late night brings. They came to the door of her room and her heart was beating so fast that she felt almost suffocated. It would be so easy, here in the night, for both of them to slip inside and shut out the world that infringed upon this yearning to be together, if only for the few hours that separated the dark hours from the dawn.

'Yes,' he breathed, 'at this moment it would be divine to enter that cool dark room with you, shutting the door behind us. But night has a way of turning into day and then I would have to leave your arms – have you the remotest conception, *ninita*, what agony it would be to leave you after loving you? I'm a man, there have been women in my life,

171

but you I will not use as a body that makes me welcome for a few hours.'

She flinched when he said this, as if he had struck at her, not because she had thought him some kind of a monk who had never felt the needs of a man, but because it hurt so much that they couldn't be lovers without shame or regret.

'I beg of you, Destine, go to your bed! Go there alone! When you awake in the morning you'll be able to face the world with unashamed eyes, as you always have. Don't you know how much your pride and dignity mean to me? You wear them like jewels, and I won't tear them from you like some thief in the night.'

'Artez – '

'No more talk, *ninita*. I can bear no more!' With a sudden strangled movement he ripped the tie loose from his shirt and turned away from her. 'I need to have a drink. Go to bed – sleep – forget!'

He strode away from her, into the shadows of the gallery, and a pang, knife-sharp, went through Destine. She was not to have even a few hours alone with him ... he was committed to Cosima and all that he left Destine was the realisation that she must leave the House of the Grilles as soon as possible.

She entered her bedroom and closed the door. She ached with a sort of grief, and for a long time she sat in the darkness on the foot of her bed, and she went over in her mind every word they had spoken, every kiss they had exchanged. It was so small a hoard of loving to see her through the empty months that lay ahead of her departure from the *casa*, and she shivered and told herself fiercely that she wouldn't have cared a damn about shame or sin, not if she could have spent this one night in his arms.

but you I will not rise as a body that makes me welcome for
a few hours.

She flinched when he said this, as if he had struck at her

CHAPTER EIGHT

THE next few days had an ominous quality about them, as if
a cloud hung persistently in the blue sky, threatening each
hour with a sudden storm.

Yet it was only an illusion, for the days were luminous
with beauty, hot and hazy with sunshine and a profusion of
flowers in the walled gardens of the *casa*.

Seeing the Don had become for Destine a torment and a
tenderness, physical and heart-stabbing. He would look at
her, and she at him, and a secret awareness would be as
palpable between them as a fine steel wire, gripping the
nerves, pulling at them, so that Destine always made some
excuse to get away before something in her manner attracted
the attention of Cosima. The greatest danger was that she
would find herself alone with him, and so she avoided all
the places where he would be on his own, the orchards, the
stables, and the loggia of Moorish design that stood alone
in a rather haunted section of the grounds, built into one of
the walls, its own walls of intricate ironwork set into plaster
its roof a small minaret rising against the palm trees.
Entrance into the loggia was by means of key-shaped open-
ings, and Destine had grown fond of the place and always
had the feeling there of a silent, fragile presence; she could
have sworn that once or twice she had caught the faint jingle
of ankle bracelets. It might be just imagination, but it
would be more than that if one afternoon the Don found her
there and they had to go through that flaming hell of keeping
out of each other's arms.

Just to see him was enough to kindle the acutest longing,
and when he smiled with a grave charm, so entirely Spanish
with its subtle shades of meaning, she wanted to cry out to

Cosima that it was wrong – so terribly wrong to play on his chivalry. He had so much more to give a woman than mere compassion, and that was all that Cosima wanted from him. Her *preux chevalier*, always protective of her and the Marquesa, and deeply involved with the running of the estate. He would make no personal demands. The marriage would be one in name only ... Destine knew that with her deepest instincts.

The knowing was a source of pain and one of acute pleasure. It meant that as a man ... purely as a man he loved *her*.

And it was that love, and the dishonour he didn't want to bring to it, that gave Destine the courage to approach the Marquesa one sunlit morning, where she sat in the *salita* with her letters. Destine quietly told her that her daughter was now as healed as she would ever be and had no real need of a private nurse any more.

'No – you must not go just yet.' The Marquesa looked aghast, as if Destine's departure would cause a setback in Cosima's recovery. 'Stay another month with us. Do let us make certain that my *carina* is really on the mend.'

'I can't stay a month, Señora Marquesa.' Panic gripped Destine, for she knew in her heart that she wanted to clutch at any excuse for staying here, so that she could see the Don each day even if she didn't dare to find herself alone with him. It would be a heavenly hell, but she had to find the strength to leave him.

'There is no justification for me to stay,' she said, and she just couldn't keep her voice from shaking a little. 'I'm just hanging around, taking payment for doing hardly anything. Cosima doesn't need me any more.'

'All the same,' the ringed hands gripped and clung to Destine's, 'remain with us and be our guest for a while. You have earned a holiday and there is no place on earth as wonderful as Xanas in high summer. The days are hot, I know, but the evenings are divine and you have worked hard

174

and had much to cope with. I know that Cosima hasn't been an easy patient, but now she seems – resigned. It's because of Artez. He's such a strong and resolute man, so very Spanish despite those strains of European blood in him. It will be a great relief when that divorce from Miguel Arandas is an assured fact – but to get back to you, Destine. You look – not exactly tired but tense and nervy. You need a rest, and you like the *casa*, don't you? It has become something of a second home to you?'

'Yes,' Destine murmured, and this was true, for the dark ghost of Manolito had faded and was almost lost in the strong living frame of the man she had grown to love. 'There never was a more beautiful house, but I really should leave at the end of the week. I want to make advances in my career and that can only be done in England.'

'This career,' the Marquesa exclaimed, 'does it never take second place to the desires that should take first place with a woman? You are much too attractive to be among the images on the shelf, and I feel a strong inclination to find a strong young Spaniard for you to fall in love with – what is the matter? Why do you catch your breath? Are you still going to tell me that you don't want the love of a man?'

Destine felt quietly shattered by the question, for never would she have believed the depth of her longing for the Spaniard who was going to become the son-in-law of this gracious woman.

'I think, Señora Marquesa, that we must accept whatever destiny has in store for us, and I believe that I am meant to be a nurse and not a wife.'

'Ah, but what a waste!' The Marquesa smiled and touched a fair strand of hair which had escaped from Destine's nape-knot. 'What pretty children you would have, and how lucky a young man would be to have you in his life, so wise and warm-hearted, and so nice to look upon. Do you still pine for your husband?'

'I shall never forget him,' Destine said, and it was true. Matthew was forever enshrined in a quiet corner of her heart, and it would always hurt that he had died so young. Had he not died, she would never have come to Xanas, and her life would be set on a contented, even course. As it was she was all at sea, terribly in love with a man she couldn't have, and not at all the outwardly composed nurse who talked of wanting only a career.

'If you go back to England the old memories will overwhelm you,' said the Marquesa. 'Won't you stay with us?'

'Until the end of the week,' Destine promised. 'Then I must go – I really must.'

'You say it in almost a desperate way.' The Marquesa looked at Destine with concern, and a tiny tinge of curiosity. 'Is it because of my nephew that you wish to leave?'

'No – ' Destine felt her heart turn over. 'Why should it have anything to do with Don Cicatrice?'

'He might have hinted that you are now redundant, with Cosima so much brighter in herself and ready to start a life anew with him – as soon as that other man is out of her life. Has he asked you to leave? He isn't a man to go all round the trees and he would tell you if he wanted you to go.'

Destine lowered her gaze in case the pain was showing in her eyes. He had told her to go, and how shocking it would be for the Marquesa if she ever knew the real reason. He was like a son to her. She loved and trusted him, and Destine wouldn't have damaged that trust for the world.

'The Don knows, as I do, that your daughter no longer needs me. He's a logical man, Señora Marquesa. Why should I be paid a salary for just hanging around your home? It's necessary for me to be needed, as it is for everyone.'

'You are needed, my dear. Be a companion to me for a while. I shall be a lonely woman when Cosima becomes the wife of Artez, for the fact must be faced that he's the type of

176

man to want his wife very close to him, especially in the first months.'

Destine glanced up sharply when the Marquesa said this, and it struck her that Cosima's mother was deluding herself when she spoke as if this marriage was going to be a close and passionate relationship. Did she really believe her own words? The wild and aching love had hold of Destine and she had to restrain the cry that rose in her, that a forceful and vibrant man was tying himself to an invalid out of a sense of honour, because the Marquesa had been good to him. There was no passion involved, on his side or Cosima's. Anyone could see it . . . anyone but a loving mother who wanted to believe that her daughter was going to be madly happy in her second marriage.

'What is it?' The Marquesa looked at Destine with a sharpening of her fine eyes. 'You seemed as if you were going to protest—has Cosima said anything to you about her feelings with regard to Miguel Arandas? Does she still imagine that she cares for him? How can she care when he left her? Artez is many times the man that Arandas is.'

'Love is not a reasonable emotion,' Destine murmured. 'Somehow or other our hearts have a will of their own and we seem defenceless when the heart chooses to love.'

'But she has agreed to marry Artez. Cosima knows that Miguel Arandas will not come back to her, and the poor child is deserving of happiness after all she has been through. Perhaps you still don't like my nephew, Destine, and feel that he will be a stern husband. Ah, I knew him as a boy. I know how affectionate he could be and I feel sure that warm vein of feeling still runs in him. He's in his middle thirties and he needs to have a wife—'

There the Marquesa broke off and bit her lip, as if for a moment she saw the striking difference between a fully active man and a woman whose lower limbs were helpless. Destine watched as the ringed hands gripped each other and

177

she knew that mother-love was at war with the painful truth.

'It will work out,' she said at last. 'Artez has the compensation of the estate, which means a great deal to him. He knows that when I die he will be in total command, and love of the land runs deep in the soul of the Spaniard. Perhaps deeper than his love of a woman.'

A cold, secret shiver ran through Destine at those words. It could be the cold truth and it had to be faced. What he felt for her might be a passing desire ... a mere masculine urge to possess her white body. But the land was eternal, and capable of giving long after a woman had passed from a man's thoughts.

'I think we have talked ourselves into a mood of depression, and that must be dispelled at once. Please to ring the service bell, Destine, and we'll have coffee with lots of thick cream. You don't care about getting plump, do you, child?'

Destine smiled, unaware of the little cloud of sadness in her blue eyes. 'Any odd ounces that I've gained will soon be burned off when I'm back on hospital duty. There isn't much time for sitting about and mooning – '

'So you are still determined to go back to your hospital work?' The Marquesa gave a sigh and toyed restlessly with the ruby ring that was companion to her wedding ring. 'I shall miss you, child. I have grown used to seeing you about the *casa*, and our little talks have always been so pleasant.'

'I shall miss you, Señora Marquesa.' Destine spoke sincerely. 'You've been very kind to me and I shan't forget you.'

They had coffee together and then Destine managed to slip away. She had a letter to write to her godmother, for she had decided that when she left Xanas she would go straight home to England and not call on the Condesa in Madrid. She would ask too many questions, and she might probe into

178

Destine's secret, and that was something to be avoided at all costs.

After the letter was written, stamped and left in readiness to be posted by one of the servants, Destine made sure that Cosima didn't require her for anything. Cosima lay reading an American magazine on the patio and she seemed hardly aware of the question. She shook her head, a trifle impatiently, and Destine quietly left her alone. There was no doubt in her mind that Cosima was lost in some impossible dream of her own, and she was equally certain that it had nothing to do with Don Cicatrice.

Heart rebellious, and nerves as tautly strung as wires, Destine changed her dress for riding trousers and a casual shirt, snatched her brimmed hat from the hook where it hung, and hurried down to the stables to Madrigal's stall. She knew that at this time of the day the Don would be in the plantations and there was no fear of running into him.

It came as a shock when he walked in on her as she was saddling up. She felt the skin of her face go tight and cold, and a tremor shook her body as he stood there against the light, a dark and almost menacing figure.

He menaced her guarded heart and shattered her self-control just by being there, a white shirt thrown open against his dark skin, his hair moistly ruffled on his brow.

'You – you startled me,' she said. 'I didn't expect to see you – '

'I was checking on one of the horses and I saw you pass by. So you are going for a ride.'

'It will be my last one at Xanas,' she said, and her fingers clenched in Madrigal's mane. 'I have told your aunt that I shall be leaving at the end of the week.'

'I see.' The words seemed to drag themselves from his throat. 'It's for the best.'

'The only thing to do.' She led her horse from the stall and was preparing to mount into the saddle when strong hands closed around her waist and lifted her. Her heart beat wildly at his touch and when she looked down at him the betrayal of her feelings was there in her eyes.

'Don't allow Madrigal to run away with you,' he said, and his lashes were heavy over his eyes as he stood there looking at her. The brimmed hat concealed her hair and she looked faintly boyish, and defiant. He didn't love her, he only wanted to make love to her, and she could surely learn to forget him if she faced up to that basic truth.

'I intend never to let anything run away with me, *señor*. I shall keep a whiphold on Madrigal, and myself.'

With those words she urged the horse into a canter, and she gazed straight ahead of her and wouldn't look back at the Don. She mustn't look back any more. It hurt too much to see his shoulders stretching the material of his shirt . . . to see his lips forming impersonal words when she wanted to be told that she meant more to him than a slim shape in his arms, firing his blood for fleeting moments in the silver-dark of a Spanish moon.

She rode away from him and he didn't call her back . . . he didn't say the words that would have consoled her.

Her departure from Xanas was arranged with smoothness and speed, and by Friday evening her suitcases and her trunk were packed, and her seat on the train was booked. She would travel as she had arrived, on the night train, and catch her plane home at an airport just outside Madrid.

'Artez must accompany you,' the Marquesa said. 'To ensure that you arrive safely at the airport.'

'There is no need.' Panic caused Destine to speak off-handedly. 'I really can take care of myself – after all, I came alone to Xanas, and I would prefer to leave on my own.'

'How independent the English are! Artez, you must insist that you go with her. It is the correct thing to do, Destine, for you are now a friend of the family. I should be most anxious about you if I thought you were all by yourself

180

with no one to look after you until you board the plane.'

'Madre, don't fuss,' drawled Cosima. 'If Destine doesn't wish to have a *dueño* in charge of her, then let the matter rest. As you say, she is English and unaccustomed to leaning on a man. That is the trouble with Latin women, we grow up believing ourselves helpless if we haven't a man in command of us. I can tell that such an attitude arouses great impatience in Destine, who is quite determined to run her own life.'

'All the same, nothing can alter the fact that Destine is a young woman.' The Marquesa had decided to be obstinate, and with a needle glittering above her frame of embroidery she stabbed her nephew with her usually gentle eyes. 'Artez, you will go with the *señora*. It will be no problem getting a seat on the train, for fewer people travel by night. I shan't rest if I know she is on her own—she is far too pretty to travel alone in Spain.'

'You hardly flatter the Spaniard, Tia.' The Don spoke with lazy amusement and took a pull at his *cigarro,* leaning there against a column of the *sala,* so placed that his scar was concealed by a falling shadow.

'On the contrary I pay him a compliment. It is no secret that the Spaniard likes a pretty face, and that, Destine, is why we guard our girls. Our men are enormously virile and therefore dangerous—Artez is smiling, as you will notice, but he knows that I speak the truth. A Spaniard will respect any woman who abides by our code, but heaven help the woman who leads him on.'

'I've never led a man on in my life.' Destine protested. 'Really, Señora Marquesa, even in the deep south women can't be expected to wear the veil and trot at the heels of a man. All that is past and done with!'

'Many things will never be of the past or done with, not while women are made differently from men. I shudder, child, to think of you alone in a railway carriage and at the

181

mercy of some man who won't respect you because you are alone. I am sure that even in England it isn't wise for a woman to travel at night without a companion. It really is a pity that our trains are so uncomfortable and overcrowded during the daytime – the only answer is that Artez escorts you. You will then have a comfortable seat and there will be no danger from anyone.'

'It is no use to argue,' he drawled, just as Destine would have argued. 'I shall come with you.'

No ... the word cried through her, as silent and as loud as the beating of her heart. She looked away from him, and the silence gathered speed and it was suddenly too late to make the protest that would have saved her from being so dangerously alone with him, shut away from the intrusive world in the dim, plushy interior of a Spanish railway compartment.

She knew that he watched her through those night-dark lashes; she knew that he waited to be denied those night-dark hours, but with all her foolish heart she wanted them. After all, they had not sought them. His aunt had insisted that he travel with her as far as the airport, and it was there that they would say goodbye.

There in the departure lounge they could kiss goodbye, and only strangers would see them. And if she wept as she turned away from him for the last time, who was there to wonder why?

'Now that is settled, let us talk about something else. May I have a light for my cigarette, *mio*?' Cosima had fitted a cigarette into a jade-green holder and now she was looking at the Don with glittering eyes, narrow and tempered as he strolled across the *sala* to the side of her sofa. A pale, brocaded sofa that set off her fragile figure in a dress that matched the holder in her hand.

'You shouldn't smoke quite so much,' he said, as he bent to her and applied his lighter to her cigarette. She just looked up at him and deliberately blew smoke into his face. Destine's nerves gave a jump and she knew at once that Cosima had wanted him to refuse his escort of the departing nurse. Love wasn't her reason, nor yet the jealousy that goes hand in hand with an intense physical love. He was her *preux chevalier* and he had no right to extend his chivalry to another woman.

Oh, God . . . Destine wanted to be gone, here and now. She wanted an end to all of it, her nerve ends anaesthetized in the busy wards of a London hospital.

'What is good for you, *mio,* is good for me.' Cosima gestured at his *cigarro.* 'I hope you aren't going to be the kind of husband who takes his own pleasures while expecting the little wife to be a sweetly submissive shadow in the background? I mean, how am I to know? The way you treat your women is a closed book to me—is it possible that there is someone close at hand who can tell me what you are like between the covers of a bed—ah, forgive me, I mean a book!'

'Cosima!' The Marquesa gave her daughter a shocked look. 'What are you saying?'

'I am sure you heard exactly what I said, Madre.' Cosima lay back against a cushion and with a delicate kind of insolence she smoked her cigarette. 'I don't think we can ignore the fact that the old wiles and intrigues haunt the very air of Xanas—did I read it in a story of Ibn H'azm, "our honey is not made for the mouth of the stranger"? But then Eve wasn't forbidden to eat the apple. It was Adam who was warned that paradise would turn to hell if he took a bite of the pale flesh with its delicate flush.'

And this time Cosima's eyes were upon Destine's face. 'Yes, Madre, you are right, she is pretty with colour high on her cheekbones, and eyes so blue they seem celestial. Are you as divinely good as you are beautiful, or is there a side to you that is tempestuous and stormy? I do believe there

183

must be, especially when I recall the sherry running like tears down the face of Fernando Castros. Such a handsome face, that makes me think of Miguel.'

'Cosima, how can you mention that man? I thought you had put him out of your mind and now you speak of him, in front of Artez. Have you no sense of propriety?' The Marquesa gave her daughter an affronted look.

'None, where Miguel is concerned. Do you imagine, Madre, that I am the light of desire in the eyes of Artez? He pities me, he doesn't love me, and I won't put him through hell – as Manolito did!'

With a sudden movement that must have caused her pain, Cosima sat up and her face was naked with a terrible truth.

'He never even whispered it in his delirium that it was Manolito who caused that fire with a cigarette he shouldn't have been smoking. I think the Obregon curse found its last resting place in Lito and I hope when he died that it finally died with him. I won't carry it on by marrying Artez – I think he should marry the one who loves him!'

Silence ... a fierce, emotional missed-beat in the heart of time, and Destine was unaware of being on her feet until she felt the tiles of the hall under the soles of her shoes. She ran, for she had to get away from these people ... she should have fled them from the very start, when she had learned that this was Manolito's house, where happiness was not allowed in.

A gush of night air struck at her, filled with the rampant perfumes of a hundred flowers climbing the walls of the enclosed patio into which she had escaped, only to find herself a prisoner as the Don came swiftly and silently on her heels, swinging her to him, taking her savagely against his hard chest.

'Why – oh, why can't you leave me alone!' She pounded at him and he didn't stop her. He allowed her to exhaust herself, until she fell silent and defeated against him

The silence was all around them, broken only by the cicadas in the treetops, chirring away in the darkness that far above them was pierced by star-points, countless pieces of silver stabbing the night sky.

'Let it end, Artez,' she whispered. 'Let me go – alone, while things can still be mended between you and Cosima. Oh, how could she have said all that – hurting her mother – hurting you! All the week I've felt it coming, a sort of storm, and now – '

'Now the storm is upon us, *ninita*, and it must be faced. There is no more hiding what we feel for each other – '

'It's a cursed love,' she gasped. 'From the very beginning! It's Manolito laughing at us from hell itself! I must go away – I will go away – you can't stop me!'

'I can't, my white witch, but I can come with you. What did you say to me? That I would never put a woman before the valley? I can and I shall, and nothing on this earth will stop me.' His arms held her with a bruising pain that swept the sufferer so close to heaven it was frightening, because it was only a fever of the moment and she couldn't surrender to it.

'You can't leave,' she said. 'Your life is here – you've given too much to the valley to ever give it up. I wouldn't ask you – '

'You ask so little that it's time someone gave you everything. Is my love enough, *ninita*? Is my life?'

'Everything that means anything to you is here,' she said, and she was almost crying. 'You belong here and you know it, and I can't stay here with you. If I had never come to Xanas you and Cosima would have been all right together – it would have made your aunt so happy.'

'A false happiness, and Tia will learn to accept that I must now live for the one whom I love.' He cradled Destine's face in his hands and he looked down deeply into her frightened eyes. 'Don't look as if I'm about to immolate myself in the

185

flames of destruction. These are the flames of love, and we leap in together – come, *queridisma*! Come!'

Together, everything left behind, the tears, the kisses on the sad cheek of his aunt, the hot south and the memories, they travelled fast through the night, heading for the possible dream.

They talked of Australia, far into the small hours, she deep in his arms as they sat there in the dim, plushy comfort of a Spanish railway compartment. Dawn came with a flaming beauty that promised all they hoped for, and looking from the window Destine said softly: 'The fire and the beauty, these are Spain – these are love.'

'These are love, my love.' And his arm held her close and looking up at him she saw the sun rising in his eyes.

ABOUT
Violet Winspear

author of "Dearest Demon".

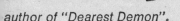

Violet Winspear's name has long been associated with the best in romantic fiction novels, and is sought after by readers who demand the very best in reading, throughout the world.

Her first Harlequin Romance, "Lucifer's Angel", was originally published in North America in 1961. Since then, Harlequin has published more than 40 other Winspear romance novels.

Violet Winspear's novels are no longer available as reprints individually, but, a number of those which are considered to be her very best works have been chosen for publication in The Harlequin Omnibus Series. The Omnibus volumes are a recent publishing event at Harlequin, and have rapidly become a very popular means of obtaining stories by favourite authors by thousands of Harlequin readers. On the following pages, we have outlined two Omnibus volumes by Violet Winspear, and some others which are available through Harlequin Reader Service.

* **Please refer to the last page for ordering information.**

"To be able to reproduce the warmly exciting world of
romance — a colourful means of escape". This was the
ambition of the young VIOLET WINSPEAR, now, a world
famous author. Here, we offer three moving stories in which
she has well and truly achieved this.

OMNIBUS (1)
Violet Winspear

containing these three exciting romances . . .

PALACE OF THE PEACOCKS (#1318) . . .
Temple Lane had saved for five years to join her
fiancee in this exotic world of blue skies and peacock
waters. Now, she must escape him. Here, we find her
in the ridiculous predicament of masquerading as a
youth on an old tub of a steamer, somewhere in the
Java Seas . . .

BELOVED TYRANT (#1032) . . .
takes us to Monterey, where high mountainous country
is alive with scents and birdsong above the blue Pacific
Ocean. As Governess at the Hacienda Rosa, Lyn Gil-
more falls victim to the tyranny of the ruthless and
savagely handsome, Rick Corderas . . .

COURT OF THE VEILS (#1267) . . .
in a lush plantation on the edge of the Sahara Desert,
Roslyn Brant tries very hard to remember her fiancee,
and her past. But, Duane Hunter refuses to believe
that she ever was engaged to marry his handsome
cousin . . .

Only once in a very long time, does an author such as Violet Winspear emerge from the hosts of writers of popular novels. Her effortless portrayal of the human emotions experienced n romantic conflict has contributed greatly to her acknowledgement as one of the very finest writers of romance known all over the world.

OMNIBUS (2)
Violet Winspear

offers three more unforgettable romances . . .

BRIDE'S DILEMMA (#1008) . . .
on the beautiful island of Ste Monique, young Tina Manson fought hard to preserve her new found happiness, the blissful state of marriage to the man whom she had loved since their very first meeting. But there was someone else who loved him, and whose endless scheming proved powerful enough to crush Tina's world . . .

TENDER IS THE TYRANT (#1208) . . .
Lauri Garner, almost eighteen years old, had such an alarming innocence about her. She had only been dancing with the great Di Corte Ballet Company a short time when she fell in love with Signor Di Corte. Unknown to Lauri, he sought only to mould her into another Prima Donna Travilla — no matter what the cost . . .

THE DANGEROUS DELIGHT (#1344) . . .
it would take a few hours before the coach could proceed. Faye was grateful for the break in her journey from Lisbon, and the chance of a short walk. To be discovered as a trespasser on the grounds of the estate of none other than the Conde Vincente of Rebelo Falcao was an innocent crime — the consequences of which were most serious . . .

* Please Refer to last page for ordering information.

INFORMATION PLEASE

Would you like to learn a little more about Harlequin, the services offered, the publications available and a host of other things which could mean a great deal more reading pleasure for you — it's very simple to find out all about us — without any obligation of course. All you have to do is send your name and address to us on the coupon below, and we'll be happy to tell you all you need to know about some of the things we do for Harlequin Readers.

In addition to some valuable information, we will also forward to you the very special "Collector's Edition" of LUCIFER'S ANGEL by Violet Winspear, **ABSOLUTELY FREE**. It's our way of saying "Thank you" for your interest in us, and in our novels.

You'll enjoy reading Violet Winspear's explosive story of the fast-moving, hard-living world of Hollywood in the 50's. It's an unforgettable tale of an innocent young girl who meets and marries a dynamic but ruthless movie producer. It's a gripping novel combining excitement, intrigue, mystery and romance.

LUCIFER'S ANGEL, Violet Winspear's first Harlequin novel has been newly printed in a special "Collector's Edition" with a new, exciting and distinctive cover design, and a complimentary copy is waiting for you — just fill out the coupon and mail it to us, to-day. SEND TO:—

VW 130 206

Here are some other **HARLEQUIN OMNIBUS** Volumes which we feel you will enjoy, written by a few of Harlequin's top authors. Each volume in the Omnibus series contains three complete, full-length Harlequin Romance stories.

* Please refer to last page for ordering information.

ESSIE SUMMERS
Bride In Flight (# 933)
Meet on My Ground (#1326)
Postscript to Yesterday (#1119)

JEAN S. MacLEOD
The Wolf of Heimra (# 990)
Summer Island (#1314)
Slave of the Wind (#1339)

ELEANOR FARNES
The Red Cliffs (#1335)
The Flight of the Swan (#1280)
Sister of the Housemaster (# 975)

ISOBEL CHACE
A Handful Of Silver (#1306)
The Saffron Sky (#1250)
The Damask Rose (#1334)

JOYCE DINGWELL
The Feel of Silk (#1342)
A Taste For Love (#1229)
Will You Surrender (#1179)

SARA SEALE
Queen of Hearts (#1324)
Penny Plain (#1197)
Green Girl (#1045)

SUSAN BARRIE
Marry A Stranger (#1043)
Rose In The Bud (#1168)
The Marriage Wheel (#1311)

JANE ARBOR
Kingfisher Tide (# 950)
A Girl Named Smith (#1000)
The Cypress Garden (#1336)

* The price of Harlequin Omnibus Volumes is only —$1.95 each.

The books outlined throughout these pages are but a few of the many romantic novels available through Harlequin Reader Service. We hope you will find them appealing, and if so, please refer to the coupon below for ordering instructions. We'll be happy to forward complete catalogue listings, detailed information and your copy of LUCIFER'S ANGEL by Violet Winspear, if you fill in and send us the coupon on the previous page.

VW 130 206